D0553731

Also by Elizabeth Starr Hill

When Christmas Comes

Evan's Corner

The Street Dancers

Broadway Chances

THE
Banjo Player

THE
Banjo Player

BY
Elizabeth Starr Hill

VIKING

VIKING
Published by the Penguin Group
Penguin Books USA Inc., 375 Hudson Street, New York, New York 10014, U.S.A.
Penguin Books Ltd, 27 Wrights Lane, London W8 5TZ, England
Penguin Books Australia Ltd, Ringwood, Victoria, Australia
Penguin Books Canada Ltd, 10 Alcorn Avenue, Toronto, Ontario, Canada M4V 3B2
Penguin Books (N.Z.) Ltd, 182–190 Wairau Road, Auckland 10, New Zealand

Penguin Books Ltd, Registered Offices: Harmondsworth, Middlesex, England

First published in 1993 by Viking, a division of Penguin Books USA Inc.

1   3   5   7   9   10   8   6   4   2

Copyright © Elizabeth Starr Hill, 1993
All rights reserved

Library of Congress Cataloging-in-Publication Data
Hill, Elizabeth Starr.
The banjo player / by Elizabeth Starr Hill.   p.   cm.
Summary: In 1888, adopted by a farming couple outside of New Orleans,
twelve-year-old orphan Jonathan must choose between security
and the excitement of performing as a musician along the river.
ISBN 0-670-84967-7
[1. Orphans—Fiction. 2. Musicians—Fiction.
3. New Orleans (La.)—Fiction.]   I. Title.
PZ7.H5514Ban 1993 [Fic]—dc20   92-41525 CIP AC

Printed in U.S.A.   Set in 11 point Palatino
Without limiting the rights under copyright reserved above, no part of this
publication may be reproduced, stored in or introduced into a retrieval system,
or transmitted, in any form or by any means (electronic, mechanical,
photocopying, recording or otherwise), without the prior written permission
of both the copyright owner and the above publisher of this book.

My thanks to

Mary Ellen Johnson

of the Orphan Train Heritage Society of America, Inc.

THE
Banjo Player

·{ 1 }··

The Orphan Train jerked and swayed, rounding a long bend in the tracks. The small boy beside Jonathan had fallen asleep briefly. Now he woke up and began to wail. His voice was almost as bad as the train whistle. Between the clacking and the swaying and the jerking and the wailing, Jonathan's temper snapped.

"Shut up that bawling, or I'll knock your head off," he told the boy tersely.

Miss Gentian, one of the Children's Aid Society agents who was traveling with them, reached across the aisle and put her hand on his arm warningly. "Hold on, there." She spoke as if to a bucking horse.

Jonathan jerked away from her. The small boy shrieked louder than ever. "He keeps yelling like that," Jonathan protested.

"We're all tired and excited. And nervous," Miss Gentian reminded him.

Jonathan couldn't deny it. His muscles—even his bones—felt cramped and tight, and his throat was knotted up. He knew nothing about his future except that he was going to a town called Laitue, in the state of Louisiana, where he might be chosen for adoption. If nobody picked him in Laitue, he would ride on to the next stop with other rejected children, and the agents would try again.

He looked out the dirty window, over the head of his bawling seatmate, and rapped his fingers on the side of his seat in the clacking rhythm of the train. The drumming fit his restlessness, gave it a form and a beat.

He could hardly imagine being part of a family. His mother had been a young Irish immigrant, too poor to keep him. She had left him at the New York Foundling Home in 1875, shortly after he was born.

At eight, he had been adopted by a couple named Dale. They had put him to work in a factory, and had treated him so harshly that he had run away, even though he had no real place to run to. He had been afraid to return to the Foundling Home, where the Dales might find him. Instead he had become one of thousands of homeless young vagrants on the New York City streets.

Jonathan whistled tunelessly, to stave off a huge melancholy. Like most of the other orphans, he had never been on a train before. At first they had all been thrilled by the unaccustomed sights and sounds of the journey. The clamor of the rails, the passing scenery, filled them with a hectic excitement. They had crowded

2

against the windows, chattering noisily about the new homes and families they hoped would want them.

But as the afternoon wore on, with Laitue still days away and Manhattan far behind, optimism died. Many of the children were leaving orphanages where they had lived for a long time. Others, like Jonathan, had survived on their own for years. All were trading the familiar for the unknown, and doubts and depression grew thick as dust in the air.

Every twenty or thirty miles, the train stopped to take on water for the boiler. One station began to look much like another.

The swerving train turned through the mountains, and pointed into a brilliant sunset sky. Jonathan tried to concentrate on it, and on his fragile hopes. The formless longing inside him—for a future that somehow suited him—seemed delicate and breakable as an egg.

In the early dusk, the train slowed for another stop. Lanterns cast their jumpy light along the platform. In the next car, a baby sobbed.

Miss Gentian and another agent opened big dinner pails and passed out apple grunts to the children. Jonathan seized an extra pastry and stuffed it into his seatmate's noisy mouth, shutting him up.

"You can walk around a bit, children. Stretch your legs," Miss Gentian announced. "But stay on the train, and no rowdiness. Don't knock any heads off, Jonathan." Her calm tone made it a pleasantry rather than a rebuke.

Jonathan leaped up. He bounced down the aisle, punching a shoulder when he recognized somebody. Many of the other passengers were strangers to him, but there were a few young peddlers and bootblacks and street performers he knew. Even though they had already greeted each other at the boarding station, Jonathan felt a need to exchange words and a friendly punch or two; to laugh with somebody.

He saw Kyle Foss at the end of the car, and made his way toward him. Like Jonathan, Kyle worked as a street performer. He and Jonathan were friendly rivals, often competing for a stretch of sidewalk space on 44th Street, in front of the rural market and saloon. Crowds of rough, good-natured shoppers passed there, and some were usually willing to part with a penny or two.

Kyle couldn't play an instrument, or shuffle his way through a dance, or even sing on key. His act depended more on nerve than talent. He simply banged pie plates together very fast, to attract a crowd, and then asked riddles.

He would start with an easy one, like, "What goes up but never comes down?"

Usually somebody in the crowd would grin and mumble, "Smoke?"

4

"What's that?" Kyle would shout. "I think I heard the right answer, but let's hear it louder!"

"*Smoke!*"

"Correct! Correct!" Kyle's green eyes would gleam; he would pull his cap off his red curls and make a bow to the clever guesser. "Very good! And now who can tell me"—the next one would be a little harder—"who can tell me what goes uphill and downhill, but never moves?"

Finally somebody might take a shot at it. "A road?"

"Excellent! A road! But I'll wager no one knows what has ears but can't hear?"

Pause. Mumble: "Must be corn."

"*What was that?*"

"*Corn!*"

"Right! Brilliant! A field of corn!"

Loosened by a trip to the saloon, people liked guessing and shouting back answers. Or maybe they just liked Kyle. Anyway, he did pretty well.

Now Jonathan punched his arm and greeted him with, "What goes on forever and never reaches Louisiana?"

"Easy. An orphan train with witty performers on board," Kyle responded at once, with his crooked grin. He lowered his voice, and added in a confidential tone, "There's something I want to talk to you about."

"Fire away."

"I don't want anybody else to hear. I thought we might make sort of a plan."

Jonathan replied in an equally guarded tone, "About what?"

Before Kyle could reply, a snickering voice at Jonathan's elbow asked, "Hey, Jonathan, how's the stolen spoon business?"

Jonathan's street act had consisted of playing tunes on his Irish tin whistle, dancing a jig, and rattling a couple of stolen spoons. Exasperated, he looked down into the sallow, scoop-cheeked face of Binch Brickett. Binch was a newsboy, a year or so younger than Jonathan, who had no more good sense than a turnip. Like the papers he sold, he found out everything and told the world.

"Shut up," Jonathan growled at him.

Kyle murmured to Jonathan, "We'll talk later."

"Right." Jonathan nodded.

"What's the secret?" Binch demanded.

"No secret. And keep quiet about the spoons. I got rid of them back in New York."

"Why?"

"To stay out of trouble, stupid. I'm through stealing." Jonathan turned away, and plopped into an empty seat beside a girl he didn't know. She gave him a confused glance.

Jonathan said brightly to her, "So it's off to a better

life and plenty of good fresh air." This was what the Children's Aid people kept telling them. "Let's hope the food is—"

The girl interrupted, "My sister was sitting here."

"She won't mind if I stay for a minute."

"Why do you want to?" she asked, tensing suspiciously.

"There's a pest I'd like to get away from." He jerked his thumb toward Binch.

"But why did you pick this seat?"

"No reason."

"You must have had *some* reason."

Jonathan sagged. In the back of his mind was an aching memory of the Sisters at the Foundling, sunny-faced, helpful. Though he hadn't seen them for years, and now would never see them again, he still missed their trust, their easy calm. He was repelled by this girl's wariness, and wished he could cut and bolt, but there was no place to go.

He rubbed his forehead, tilting his cap back, and said rudely, "I didn't pick this seat, it's just the nearest empty one. I certainly didn't pick *you* especially. I'll leave in a minute."

"Oh. All right." She leaned her head against the seat and looked out the window. They were silent, as the others in the car continued their uproar.

Then she said, "My sister and I probably won't be

placed together. Boys are more needed than girls. Two girls aren't likely to be needed by anybody."

Jonathan knew all the siblings hoped to be placed together. He realized she was expressing an awful fear, and the thought made him feel kindlier toward her. He mumbled, "We can't know what'll happen or who'll want us."

"That's true." Her face was composed, but pale. She had a light sprinkle of freckles across a turned-up nose. Her long brown hair was tied back with a pink ribbon, crumpled now, though the Children's Aid people had tidied up all the children before the journey.

Jonathan added, "Anyway, we'll have families of our own, at last." Many of the orphans said this to each other, over and over. He had never said it before; he remembered the Dales too well; but it sounded cheerful.

She looked at him directly. Her eyes were shadowed; he couldn't tell what color they were. To Jonathan, the jumbled bleakness of their pasts seemed to flow between them, unknown, but somehow understood. He was afraid she would cry, but she didn't.

"My sister is my family," she said.

Jonathan could find no answer to this.

After a minute, she asked, "What's your name?"

"Jonathan."

"I'm Marguerite."

In the aisle, a small girl shoved past Binch Brickett and told Jonathan belligerently, "That's my seat."

He got up. The train squealed and gave a forward jolt, almost pitching him off his feet. He regained his seat. So did everybody else. With much jerking and jolting, the train started again.

·{ **2** }·

Traveling through the night, Jonathan looked out at clusters of street lamps that marked one small town after another. Most of the streets were nearly deserted.

He thought of spring evenings in New York. The girl who sold bunches of violets on Fifth Avenue did a brisk business after dark. Jonathan himself had always welcomed evening. It was a generous time, a lavish time.

He put aside the memory of how keen his hunger had been sometimes. During last month's blizzard, he might have frozen or starved to death if the Children's Aid Society hadn't rescued him. Still, he longed for the city.

The train jolted and swerved around a bend. A young boy tumbled into the aisle, which made everybody laugh. Somebody started singing a popular circus song, got the tune wrong, tried again.

Jonathan fished in the bundle that rested beside him on the seat. It contained a few extra items of clothing from the Children's Aid people, and a Bible with his name on it in gold. Each orphan had been given one. Also in the bundle was his oldest and best-loved possession—his tin whistle.

He pulled it out and blasted a clear note to get everybody's attention. Then he piped the rollicking tune of the circus song. His mood bounced up with the music. Soon the whole carload was following his lead, singing giddily, "He flies through the air with the greatest of ease . . . The daring young man on the flying trapeze. . . ."

Ah, well, Jonathan thought, *this isn't so bad! We're on our way!*

Around noon the next day, the orphans were taken off the train just for an hour, to have a meal in a station restaurant. For Jonathan the treat was tempered by discomfort, as other patrons stared at them. While he was eating his soup, eyes on the tablecloth, he caught the whispered words, "Orphan Train."

He sensed that he and his companions were objects of curiosity, even of pity, and the knowledge boiled in him. Jonathan usually presented himself as brassy and capable; a lively New Yorker, powered by the fun and vigor of the city. Even when he had been nearly starving, he had depended on a jig and a tune to see him through. No hard-luck stories for Jonathan, and no pity either, if he could help it.

He forced himself to meet the inquisitive glances, and stared them down stonily.

Kyle Foss signaled to him from across the table. Jonathan remembered they had agreed to talk privately. As soon as the meal was over, they walked together to the station platform.

"Before we left New York, I found out something," Kyle confided in an undertone.

"What?" demanded little big-ears Binch Brickett, slithering up from nowhere.

Kyle said sharply, "Get away, Binch. It's no business of yours."

Binch retreated briefly, though Jonathan had a feeling he was nearby, tiresome as a mosquito. No matter how often you swatted him off, he returned to madden you again.

Kyle explained that he had stayed in the Children's Aid shelter in New York for a couple of weeks before the Orphan Train left. One morning he had overheard two officials talking, and had learned from the conversation that most of the families applying for orphans were farmers. There were a few shopkeepers and restaurant owners as well. But one set of applicants was different. They lived on a boat, on the Mississippi River, and they wanted a boy around twelve or thirteen.

"A boat? What kind of a boat?" Jonathan asked.

"I don't know. I wouldn't have paid much attention, except one man said, 'Sounds as if Kyle Foss or Jonathan Dale would fill the bill.' "

"Us? Why us, especially? I don't know anything about boats."

"Neither do I." Kyle shrugged. "It's a mystery. But I was thinking—" His keen green eyes glowed with conspiracy. "If it would be a good home for *one* of us, why not for *both* of us? Maybe we could be adopted together!"

Jonathan's sense of adventure rose. He and Kyle, brothers and workmates! Even swabbing decks, or setting sails, or whatever you had to do on a boat, would be tolerable—more than tolerable—with Kyle to share jokes with.

"But—what makes you think they'd take both of us?" he asked.

Kyle replied, "Well, we'll just have to try our best, won't we? Stick together when the applicants are choosing."

"Try to put in a few words about how we love boats," Jonathan improvised with a grin.

"Right. How much we *both* love boats," Kyle emphasized.

"*I* like boats pretty good," Binch put in from behind them.

Jonathan tried to give him a push, but missed. Binch was agile.

Miss Gentian called, "We're boarding the train, now. Stay together. *Peacefully*. Please."

Racketing over the rails again, the children played word games, told jokes, sang songs; anything to pass the time. Jonathan piped lively melodies: "Turkey in the Straw," "The Blue Tail Fly," "Camptown Races."

But as another night came on, everyone fell silent. Spirits sank with the setting sun.

Jonathan's thoughts returned to boats. He had been on ferries a few times, and once, on a rare outing with the Dales, for a ride in a pleasure gondola on the Central Park lake. It had been a warm summer day, the sun thick as ladled honey across the water.

He never wanted to see the Dales again. But the lake . . . the park . . . the gondolas . . . they were gone, too. His memories seemed rimmed in sorrow and in loss.

··{ 3 }··

Half an hour before the train was due to arrive at Laitue, Miss Gentian wakened her charges, gave them a sketchy breakfast, and neatened them up. "Button your jacket," she told Jonathan distractedly. "Where's your cap?"

Jonathan found the cap and jammed it on his head. It was early in the morning, and pouring rain outside. Nothing could be seen through the streaked windows except a blurry gray greenness. Jonathan supposed they must be riding through fields at the outskirts of town.

He had only a dim idea of what would happen next. As Miss Gentian wiped noses and retied hairbows, he asked her gruffly, "Families going to be looking us over soon?"

She was tired, as they all were, but she smiled. "Yes. They're probably waiting at the meetinghouse. The train's a little late."

Jonathan assumed an attitude of blustering humor. "Maybe nobody'll come."

"Oh, don't worry. There've been flyers distributed,

and posters put up. We have a lot of applicants for children. They'll be there."

"To pick and choose."

"Yes." She gave him a quick glance and said warmly, "You're tall and healthy, Jonathan. You'd make a good farm worker, and many of our applicants are country folk. You'll be chosen."

A farm worker?

He ventured, "I heard one family lives on a boat."

"Oh, is that right?" she answered vaguely; whether in real ignorance, or to avoid discussion, Jonathan couldn't tell. "Well, *someone* will take you, wait and see."

He nodded. After nights of interrupted sleep and joggling, he felt slightly sick. The possibility of being adopted along with Kyle seemed remote, in the rainy gray light of morning. After all, there were brothers and sisters on the train; people who, by rights, shouldn't be separated. Marguerite and her little sister. Others. Yet they had no assurance they could stay together.

A farm worker.

At the Foundling Home, he had read about the old slave auctions in New Orleans, when black people had been sold like cattle. Since the Civil War had ended, slavery was illegal, but it seemed to him that this was not so different.

As though reading his mind, Miss Gentian added earnestly, "Every family has to agree to provide a good home, Jonathan."

He nodded again. Privately he wondered if the Dales, too, had promised a good home.

The train jerked and slowed, approaching the station. Jonathan's stomach lurched with it. He decided he would never like trains. They took away your freedom, sped you where you didn't want to go, into situations you didn't want to be in. The old urge to flee rose strongly in him. Maybe he could get away from Miss Gentian at the station, and disappear in the streets of Laitue.

But he knew he wouldn't do this. Confused though his hopes were, the thin-shelled, formless longing for a better life still waited inside him, unbroken.

The train pulled into the station and squealed to a stop. Jonathan stood up and stretched his cramped legs. To dispel his nervousness, he gave his small seatmate a friendly punch on the arm, and asked him, "Got your cap?"

The boy nodded drearily. His cap was, in fact, on his head. Probably he was already working at making a good impression.

Well, smart idea. Jonathan picked up his bundle and joined the crowd in the aisle. He had watched sophisticated gentlemen often enough. There was no reason he couldn't take on their manners. He greeted Marguerite and her sister, even Binch, with new cordiality. From now on, he would be the kind of a person a fine family might choose to adopt. He wished he had done it sooner. He had wasted years, when he might have been turning himself into a model of excellence.

At the station platform, open umbrellas glistened like dark flowers above the bustle of travelers. Drawling voices murmured, different from rapid New York voices. The close Southern air clothed Jonathan at once in a warm, damp sheen.

Grasping his bundle, he swung to the platform and helped his seatmate down the steep steps. Then he reached to give Marguerite a hand. He flourished the gesture, as he had seen gentlemen do when assisting a lady from a carriage. She rewarded him with a wary glance, planted her boots firmly on the iron steps, and jumped down by herself.

Her little sister was next. "Help *me*," she demanded.

Jonathan swung her down.

In the clutter of freight and hurrying people, the orphans milled hectically for a minute. Mr. O'Toole, a Children's Aid agent, herded them into a line and led them quickly from the station into the street. The snorting of horses, the clatter of carriages and buggies and wagons and carts, surrounded them. Jonathan looked around quickly, trying to gauge the town. The buildings were small, compared to many in New York, and the roads narrow. He couldn't tell much more about the place, in the drizzling rain.

He tried to join Kyle Foss up ahead, but Miss Gentian stopped him. "Keep in line," she said firmly.

As they tramped up the rain-soaked street, they passed two women sheltered in a shop doorway. "Oh, those must be the orphans," one said, gaping after them. "My land, what a pathetic crew!"

Jonathan flushed painfully. He hadn't been so neat and clean in years. The words seared through him. He saw himself and his companions as this woman did, rumpled, in ill-fitting clothes, not really knowing how to behave. He was humiliated. He longed to tell her to shut up.

To his hidden delight, Marguerite's little sister shouted, "Sew up your mouth, you old snake, before toads fall out."

Miss Gentian hurried the child along, shushing her.

"Hiss, hiss, hiss, old snake!" the girl shouted, unquenchable.

"Mercy goodness, listen to *that*," a shocked response came from an onlooker.

More comments followed them: "I read in the paper that the orphans were arriving today."

"Must be why the road in front of the meeting-house is so crowded."

"Yes, people coming to take them in, poor little souls." And in a lower voice, "I wouldn't take a chance on them, would you?"

"No, never. I've heard that some of the farmers get a lot of work out of them, but I wouldn't risk having one around."

Jonathan wiped rain off his cheeks with the back of his hand, looking straight ahead. In New York, a three-headed elephant would have caused less comment than this. If this was small-town life, he was glad he had been spared it.

A group of boys suddenly danced up beside him, taunting, "Beggars! Orphans! Tramps!"

Jonathan stepped from the line and tried to punch the nearest boy, who darted out of reach. The others laughed and jeered. Jonathan's bundle fell into the wet street. Binch Brickett snatched it up—whether to save it or steal it, Jonathan never knew. He grabbed it back, and let the jeering boys go their way.

The next block was jammed with horses and wag-ons and carts, tied up in front of a plain wooden build-ing. Jonathan and the others quickened their pace, realizing this must be the meetinghouse. Following Mr. O'Toole, they clattered up its wooden steps.

··{ **4** }··

The meetinghouse smelled of damp clothes on a warm day. Several rows of rain-soaked men and women sat in wooden chairs, facing an empty platform in the front. As the orphans trooped in, these people turned eagerly. Many smiled and waved. Jonathan heard one kind voice say, "Welcome," and was encouraged.

Binch, quickly seeking an advantage, turned to the greeter and waved, as though the welcome were meant especially for him.

Mr. O'Toole climbed to the low platform and faced the crowd, beckoning to the orphans to join him. As they sprang up, Jonathan and Kyle maneuvered to stand side by side. Roy Shafer, a large, good-natured boy who sometimes worked as a trash picker in Central Park, stood on Jonathan's other side.

"Good morning, ladies and gentlemen," Mr. O'Toole said. "Thank you for coming. I know your reward will be great, if it results in giving homes to these fine boys and girls." He went on like that for several minutes, extolling the orphans' health, strength, and general character.

"He should be selling horses," Kyle hissed. "He'd make a fortune."

Jonathan smothered a burst of jittery laughter. He looked down at the people sitting below. Most were very plainly dressed, the women with homespun shawls pulled around their cotton dresses, the men in work shirts and overalls. He couldn't tell if there were any sailors. It seemed to him that sailors would be weather-beaten and sunburned, but many people here looked that way; it was so hot, it felt like the middle of summer. Already Jonathan was beginning to sweat in his woolen city suit and high collar.

Mr. O'Toole wound up his palaver. "Well, ladies and gentlemen, this is the moment you've been waiting for. At last each of you will have the opportunity to judge these splendid youngsters, and to decide if you want to accept one or more into your own home."

"Remember what we planned," Kyle whispered to Jonathan.

Jonathan nodded, scanning the crowd again.

Mr. O'Toole turned to the orphans. "Children, please tell these good folk your names and ages. You begin, Roy."

"Yes, sir." He cleared his throat. "Big Roy Shafer—" There was some kindly laughter, which threw him off for a moment. He added defensively, "That's what they call me."

"Go ahead." Mr. O'Toole smiled.

"Fourteen years old," Roy ended, twisting his cap in his hands. He added, "I'm very strong."

Jonathan was next. He spoke briskly. "Jonathan Dale, twelve years old."

Kyle was equally brisk. "Kyle Foss, thirteen years old."

"Binch Bickett, ten years old, wiry and tough, not a big eater—"

"That's enough, Binch," Mr. O'Toole interposed.

Marguerite was next. She didn't speak for a few seconds. Jonathan glanced at her. She was standing very straight and pale, holding the hand of her young sister. When she finally said her name, her voice was frail. "Marguerite Coye, eleven."

"Eugenie Coye, eight years old."

As it went on down the line, Jonathan became aware of a middle-aged man and woman in work clothes, in the second row. Their eyes fixed first on Eugenie, then moved to him. They nudged each other, exchanged a whispered consultation, then focused on him again. Jonathan's heart began to thud.

When all the orphans had identified themselves,

Mr. O'Toole told the prospective families, "No doubt you'll want to talk among yourselves. Please ask the children, or me, any questions you wish."

Murmurs of discussion swept the hall. Some men and women surged forward to speak to Mr. O'Toole or Miss Gentian. A few very young children were carefully considered, chosen, and carried out by their new families.

A man with red hair walked up to the platform and told Kyle good-naturedly, "Say, you look a lot like me, son." There was general laughter; Kyle's curly hair was almost the same color as his.

"Is that his real father?" a tiny girl asked loudly. The younger orphans especially were always talking about real mothers and fathers.

"No, he's just joking," Miss Gentian explained hurriedly.

"I love boats," Kyle told the man rather desperately, taking a shot in the dark.

"Me, too," Binch said quickly.

"Boats?" The man looked puzzled. "That so?"

Wrong one, Jonathan thought.

The middle-aged man and woman who had been scrutinizing Jonathan now turned their attention back to Marguerite's sister. "Would you kindly step forward, little girl?" the man asked in his soft Southern voice.

24

"Me?" asked Eugenie.

"Yes, please."

Eugenie let go of Marguerite and moved stiffly to the edge of the platform, her round face suddenly frightened. Her dark coat was too long. Her black stockings wrinkled around her ankles. Even the bonnet perched above her brown braids was too large for her. Her small hands curled around the bundle containing her Bible and other possessions.

The middle-aged man and woman got up quietly and came to stand directly in front of her at the low platform.

"I need a little girl to help me in the house." The woman spoke and smiled reassuringly.

Eugenie, her face agonized, did not answer.

A girl. So they had decided against him already, Jonathan thought, with a bitter twist of disappointment.

He paid scant attention to the rest of the exchange with Eugenie, but started searching through the gathering for someone else who might show interest in him. He had a sharp eye for prospects in any audience, and smiled alertly whenever he met a measuring glance.

The middle-aged couple turned to him. "Can you read, boy?" the man asked, in an easy voice.

"Oh, yes, sir. And I can write, and do sums."

"And you, Eugenie." The man smiled at her. "Can you read?"

"No," she whispered.

"Maybe a few words? Can you write your name?"

She shook her head.

The man and woman moved away slightly and conferred. Try as he would, Jonathan couldn't hear what they were saying.

Finally the man spoke to him again. "My name's Walter Tilden. I'm a tenant farmer. You know what that is?"

"No," Jonathan admitted.

The man's eyes were blue, nested in white crinkles from squinting at the sun. The rest of his face was deeply tanned. "My wife and I"—he indicated the woman by his side—"we rent some land and farm it. We're tryin' to make a go of it, but it's mighty hard."

"Oh," Jonathan said.

"We have no children to help us," Mr. Tilden went on. "We had a daughter, but she died of the cholera."

Jonathan swallowed, not knowing how to reply. But again the Tildens were looking at Eugenie. He had a sinking feeling she was the one they were really interested in.

"It was years ago, and we've been wantin' to have other children," Mr. Tilden told the little girl, who looked at him with a round scared face. "But the Lord hasn't blessed us."

"Until today." Mrs. Tilden put her hand on her husband's arm, as though imploring him to agree. "Until today, Walter."

"That's right. Until today." The man drew a deep breath and let it out, as though coming to a major decision. With emotion in his eyes, he said to Eugenie, "If you—and Jonathan here—would come home with us and help us out on the farm—be our children—we would be blessed."

Jonathan's thoughts tumbled in confusion. He was aware of Kyle beside him, and of the hopeless plan they had made. It seemed ridiculous now. It had nothing to do with this reality in the steamy-smelling hall at Laitue.

He was being offered a home—or rather, Eugenie was, and he along with her. A confused kind of gladness and relief poured over him.

Before he could respond, Eugenie cried out, "Me? But what about my sister?"

Jonathan looked at Marguerite. On her pale face, the freckles stood out like sprinkled nutmeg. Her eyes were huge, glistening with tears, but she didn't make a sound.

Eugenie began to shriek. Dropping her bundle, she

grabbed her sister with both arms, crying, "Take her, too! Take her, too!"

Mr. O'Toole and Miss Gentian hustled over. Throughout the hall there was a brief stir of attention, sighs of pity. But in a moment, the members of the gathering had returned to their own concerns.

Eugenie kept screaming. Miss Gentian pried her from Marguerite as gently as she could. Mr. Tilden was protesting, "We can't take more, just a girl and a boy."

Her voice sorrowful, Miss Gentian urged Eugenie, "Be brave, my dear. Others will have to be, too."

Finally Eugenie quieted enough to be lifted from the platform by Mr. Tilden. Jonathan picked up her dropped bundle and held it with his own. Mrs. Tilden smiled and extended a hand to him. He took it and hopped down, leaving Kyle, Binch, all the others.

The pain of separation swept over him, cutting like a knife. He was leaving his friends, his only friends.

He looked back over his shoulder. Still on the platform, Kyle watched him, green eyes desolate. Binch was talking to a stocky couple, and paid no attention to Jonathan's departure. Big Roy Shafer was answering questions put to him by the red-headed man.

Jonathan's gaze moved on to Marguerite. She was not crying, as Eugenie was, but stood motionless, silent, as though turned to marble.

·{ 5 }·

Jonathan jounced along between the Tildens on the wooden seat of their old wagon. Eugenie slept in the carry-flat in back. Pulled by a stocky farm horse, the wagon bumped over muddy, rutted country roads.

It had stopped raining. The sun cracked through shifting clouds, bringing up mist from the wide flat landscape. They had left Laitue, and were traveling deep into farm country.

The Tildens had explained that their farm was in Meander Creek, west of New Orleans. It would be a long ride in the heat.

"Take off that jacket, son," Mr. Tilden suggested.

Jonathan did, and felt better, though the strangeness of the place made him uneasy. When he had left New York, its trees were still nearly bare in the cool of April. Here the landscape was lush and green. Unknown birds with long plumes roosted in the trees. An occasional wooden shack or barn or farmhouse showed among the steaming fields, but no other buildings.

Field workers were picking strawberries, hoeing

cotton, setting out young tobacco plants. At first the Tildens were eager to explain their activities to Jonathan, but his unease seemed to spread to them. The talk died out.

Eugenie wakened briefly, wailed, "I want my sister," and fell asleep again. They rode on in silence.

The sun grew stronger. Jonathan became terribly hungry and thirsty. He asked, "Will we get there by dinnertime?"

"Oh, yes." Mrs. Tilden looked down at him with her thin smile. "You like crayfish?"

"Anything," Jonathan replied truthfully.

"Crayfish is mighty good, especially the way Ma makes it," Mr. Tilden put it.

Jonathan didn't know who he was talking about. "Ma?"

Mrs. Tilden explained hesitantly, "We don't know how you'd feel about this, Jonathan, but we hoped you might want to call us Ma and Pa Tilden. Unless you still have lovin' feelings toward—toward some other Ma and Pa."

Jonathan's mother flashed into his mind, as he always imagined her—pretty, with dark hair and blue eyes like his own, and wild-rose cheeks, fresh from the air of Ireland. He pictured her high-stepping through the shamrocks, her laughter bouncing from the green, green hills. A lump rose in his throat.

Then there was Sister Mary Perpetua at the Foundling Home, hiking up the skirts of her long habit just above her stout ankles, eyes merry behind her glasses, showing him how to dance a jig. He remembered when she had given him the tin whistle, and how quickly he had learned to play it. "When I grow up, I'm going to be in a show!" he had exclaimed joyfully.

"Indeed you will! You will, Jonathan, with the Lord's help!" she had assured him.

Next he thought of Mr. Cassidy. The aged grocer had helped him out often, during his first year on the streets. He had given him wilted vegetables and day-old bread, always with a smile and a pat on the shoulder.

Later, after Mr. Cassidy died and the grocery was left empty, Jonathan and a pack of other homeless children slept in its crumbling cellar. For a long while, Jonathan had dreamed that Mr. Cassidy was still upstairs, ready to pass out leftovers with his careful, gnarled hands. . . .

He realized Mr. and Mrs. Tilden were waiting anxiously for him to answer. He cleared his throat. "I have no other loving feelings."

"Well, we'd be right pleased if you was to call us that, then," Mr. Tilden said.

Jonathan nodded. He couldn't bring himself to say anything more; didn't even know exactly how he felt about it. He had met the Tildens only a little over an hour ago, and would have been content to call them Mister and Missus for a while.

The Tildens both made gratified sounds. In a whispery voice, Ma said, "So we're a real family." She pulled a handkerchief from her pocket and wiped her eyes, adding, "And little Eugenie will do like you do, Jonathan. I know it."

Jonathan couldn't see the logic to this. "Think so?" he asked dubiously.

"Well, you're her big brother now," Ma Tilden told him with a tremulous smile.

Jonathan was certain this was rushing it. Though he was only slightly acquainted with Eugenie, he doubted she would take any hints from anybody—or that she was ready for a ma, and a pa, and a big brother.

He wondered if the Tildens had any more relationships in mind for them—or any name changes. Would he have to be a Tilden now? He hoped not. Although he had hated the Dales, Jonathan Dale was his legal name, and he wanted to keep it.

Haltingly, he asked if this would be all right.

"Why, sure," Pa said. "You're indentured to us, son, but we haven't signed the adoption papers yet. With older youngsters like you, they suggest a sort of a trial period, you know?"

"I don't understand," Jonathan said.

"Well, you live with us and work for us, we give you food and shelter, but it don't have to be permanent."

"Though we *expect* it will be," Ma put in.

"But what if it *is* permanent?" Jonathan asked. "What about my name?"

"Why, that's up to you," Pa said. "If you take to farm life and want to stay with us, we can talk about it again in a few months. How's that?"

Jonathan wondered what would happen to him if he *didn't* want to stay. Here he was, in Louisiana, without another prospect in the world. He lifted his head proudly, to give himself courage. "Fair enough," he said in a businessman's voice.

The mist cleared, and it kept getting hotter. Pa put on a wide straw hat, and Ma a sunbonnet. Jonathan's cap did nothing to ward off the sun. His skin tightened, burned by the hot rays. His feet swelled and ached inside his boots and heavy woolen stockings; the boots were too small, anyway. His body prickled with sweat.

When the sun was almost directly overhead, Ma said, "There's the spring, Pa. Let's stop for lunch."

Lunch! They were going to have lunch! Even more wonderful, water gushed from a spring in the bank beside the road. It splashed into a roadside watering trough for horses.

Pa stopped the wagon in the shade of a huge tree. Jonathan jumped out. Cupping his hands above the trough, he drank handful after handful of the delicious, ice-cold springwater. He splashed it over his head and face, dousing his neck and shoulders, soaking his shirt. He shook his head, sending drops flying in all directions.

Ma chuckled. "You look like Barney now."

"Who's Barney?"

"Our farm dog. He jumps in the pond, then when he comes out it's shake, shake, shake, like that."

Pa tethered the horse and let it drink from the trough, then tied a nosebag of oats over its mouth so it could eat. Ma spread a checkered cloth on the grass and unpacked lunch for the rest of them. Jonathan saw cornbread, biscuits and jam, a wedge of cheese.

He darted over and grabbed a biscuit. He was about to stuff it in his mouth when he noticed Ma's dismayed face. He dropped it, ashamed of his grabby manners.

"We'll be eatin' in a minute. Seems like you could wait that long," Ma told him.

"Sure thing," Jonathan replied, mortified.

"We best wake up Eugenie." Pa lifted the girl from the wagon. She rubbed her eyes, blinking. Her face was red with sunburn. "Ready for lunch?" he asked her gently.

She nodded.

Ma and Pa led her and Jonathan in different directions, to "do the necessary" behind a hedgerow. Then they all sat on the grass around the checkered cloth, and Ma passed out food. Jonathan couldn't help wolfing the cheese and biscuits. He always crammed in as much as he could hold. Eugenie ate slower, but at a steady pace.

When he was full, Jonathan looked around at the green bank with the sparkling spring gushing from it, and at the great tree that shaded them with its wide crooked limbs. He pointed to the long gray stuff that hung like cobwebs from its branches. "What's that?"

"Spanish moss," Pa answered. "Your bedtick at home is stuffed with it. Makes right good sleepin'."

Ma turned to Eugenie. "You'll have the same kind of bed, little sister. Rope, with a nice soft moss tick on it."

The little girl did not respond. She was drinking from a tin cup of water Pa had given her, staring into space.

"That water's mighty good, isn't it?" Ma asked encouragingly.

Eugenie didn't answer.

"I always say there's nothin' like springwater." Pa smacked his lips.

"Sure beats sour milk or cheap beer," Jonathan joked loudly to lighten the atmosphere.

Both Tildens looked at him reprovingly. Eugenie giggled.

"Not that it's anything *like* sour milk," Jonathan stammered in horror, realizing his mistake. "And I've certainly never tasted—that is, I've—" He broke off in hasty confusion.

Ma passed the biscuits again. Her lean face seemed to grow longer and more dispirited. Soon they packed up the picnic things and traveled on.

⸱⟨ **6** ⟩⸱

Hours later, the horse clopped over a narrow bridge and across a winding stream. Pa said, "This here is Meander Creek."

A large, shining-white house came into view. It had white pillars in front and a fancy lantern hanging above the door. A row of trees, straight as soldiers, lined the drive leading from the house to the road.

Awed, Jonathan asked, "That's your house?"

With a deprecating laugh, Pa shook his head. "No, nothin' like it." He explained that much of the land around Meander Creek belonged to Mr. Ashley, whose home this was. "We just lease our place from him. It's a quarter mile further on."

They rounded a bend in the rutted road. Now Jonathan could see a small gray farmhouse with batten shutters, its porch sagging. There was a barn nearby, and a tumbledown henhouse. Cows stood ankle-deep in a shallow pond in front of the house, accompanied by long-legged birds.

A lumbering dog ambled forward, tail wagging. Jonathan said, "I guess that's Barney."

"That's him," Pa affirmed. The horse and wagon halted. Jonathan glanced at Eugenie, who was taking covert peeks at the farmhouse, the dog, the cows.

They climbed down from the wagon, each carrying their little bundle of possessions. Pa unhitched the horse.

Eugenie stopped, sniffing. "This place smells."

"I reckon that's the cows you smell," Pa said. He sounded slightly distressed. "You get used to it."

He showed them where the orchard was, and the outhouse, and the barn. "Guess you city younguns don't get much chance to go wadin', so wash up in the pond," he added hospitably. "Then come on inside. It's near suppertime."

Eugenie and Jonathan exchanged unhappy glances. They set their bundles on the bank and took off their boots and stockings.

"Do you think there are snakes in there?" Eugenie asked in a trembling voice.

"I don't see any," Jonathan replied.

Peering down into the murky water, they waded up to their ankles, mud oozing between their toes.

"I'm clean enough," Eugenie quickly decided.

"Right," Jonathan agreed in relief. They joined Ma and Pa in the kitchen. Barney had to stay out until he finished shaking and splattering.

The cramped house consisted of a kitchen and three

sleeping rooms, all on one floor. There was a big iron wood-burning cookstove in the kitchen. A table was set for supper. Jonathan noticed a framed embroidered picture of a weeping willow, with a gravestone that read: "*Sarah Ellen Tilden, 1880–1885. The trumpet shall sound, and the dead shall be raised.*"

He realized this was a mourning picture for the Tildens' little girl. If she had lived, she would be eight years old, like Eugenie.

Ma said, "Sarah Ellen's room is going to be yours, Eugenie. *You're* our daughter now."

She and Pa led the way to an open door. Eugenie hesitated in the doorway, clutching her bundle. Looking past her, Jonathan saw a colorful patchwork quilt on the bed, and a cornhusk doll on a child-sized window seat. Pictures of toys, cut out of a mail-order catalogue, decorated the walls. A bunch of wispy wildflowers bloomed in a blue glass vase.

Jonathan hoped Eugenie wouldn't say anything mean, and she didn't. "Flowers," she commented. The Tildens seemed pleased that she had noticed.

Jonathan's room was the smallest. It had only a rope bed, a wooden chest for clothes, and a table. A strip of sticky flypaper hung beside the one narrow window. Dead and dying insects were stuck to it like raisins, some still buzzing fretfully.

"Set your bundles down, younguns, and we'll eat," Pa said.

In the kitchen, Ma said, "Now, you watch how I do, Eugenie." She seasoned a cauldron of boiling water with garlic, chopped onions, lemon, and red pepper. Then she took a bucket of live crayfish, which had been kept during the day in the creek water they were caught in, and poured them into the bubbling brew.

"Ugh." Eugenie shuddered, turning away in disgust.

Soon delicious cooking smells filled the air, and they all sat at the table.

A black field hand, introduced as Millard, came in to eat with them. He greeted Eugenie and Jonathan with a warm smile and a cordial, "How you doin'? Just about wore out, I reckon. I heard you-all had a mighty long trip."

"Too long," Jonathan told him eagerly, recognizing a sociable soul when he met one. "I'll never ride a train again."

"That right? I'm just the opposite," Millard declared. "I love trains! Ain't been on 'em much, though."

They compared train experiences, while Ma served up collards with salt pork, a dish of boiled potatoes, and the supreme dish, a big platter of red-shelled crayfish. There were fried hush-puppies, too, to share with Barney.

Jonathan waited till the others had helped themselves. Then he heaped his own plate. He pulled the crayfish shells off as he saw the grown-ups do. This wasn't as easy as it looked. If you weren't careful, you ended with mangled shells and nothing to eat. Still, the morsels he managed to extract were delicious, though peppery.

He swallowed a large number of them, and started on a second helping.

"See?" Pa said, looking pleased. "I told you you'd like 'em, fixed Ma's way."

"I do." Jonathan munched on.

"Mighty good, Miz Tilden," Millard complimented her. The field hand popped the zesty morsels into his mouth nonstop, zipping the shells off with incredible ease. "Once I was to the crayfish festival in Breaux Bridge?" he related in his upswinging Southern drawl. "By Atchafalaya Swamp?"

"I was there once," Pa put in. "Cajun country."

"At the festival, they had a crayfish race," Millard went on. "Put six of 'em on this big round wooden table. Circles painted on it. They set them crayfish inside the smallest circle, in the middle, like it was the bull's-eye." The succession of shellfish into his mouth never slowed. "And a lot of us bet on which one would climb across all them circles first."

"Huh," Ma commented interestedly, chewing steadily.

Millard helped himself to more red-shelled heaps from the platter and went on, "Seemed like them crayfish didn't want to get started at first. Then they went this way, then that way."

Jonathan could tell Millard was dragging out the drama of it. He grinned, enjoying the black man's storytelling style.

"What happened in the end?" Eugenie asked.

"The one I bet on was the winner! Got started, made up its mind, and *zoom*, right across the table!"

"Huh!" Ma said again.

"What'd you win?" Jonathan asked, happy about the way the incident came out.

"Free dinner at the crayfish boil. All I could eat."

"Why did you choose that one to bet on?" Eugenie asked.

"Just luck."

"You must have had *some* reason," Eugenie insisted.

"Guess he was the biggest," Millard answered agreeably.

Jonathan thought of how Marguerite, on the train, had asked, "Why did you choose this seat?" and then argued, "You must have had *some* reason." It intrigued him that the two sisters, in two different situations, had shown such similar turns of mind. Was this the way families were? Would he and Eugenie grow more alike, as time went on? Or would they both become more and more like the Tildens?

He noticed that the grown-ups adroitly slipped the skins off their potatoes and forked them onto a newspaper in the middle of the table, along with the crayfish shells. He had never wasted a potato skin in his life, but he attacked the skinning job determinedly. The potato rolled. His fork clattered. He grabbed at them with both hands, almost undone by difficulties.

Unlike him, Eugenie didn't seem to care what anybody else did. She ate her potato, skin and all, and went to bed right after supper.

Millard left, too, for the unpainted wooden cabin where he slept. It was barely visible through a scrub of pines, out beyond the barn.

Silently Ma cleaned up the dishes and set the table for breakfast. Jonathan helped her, nervously copying everything she did. She gave him a bleak smile. "Seems the girl should be givin' me a hand, not you."

"I don't mind." He tried to add "Ma," but the word stuck in his throat.

"I reckon she's just bashful."

Remembering Eugenie before she had been parted

from Marguerite, Jonathan didn't think bashful described her, but it seemed to be what Ma Tilden wanted to believe. "I reckon." The unfamiliar phrase was strange in his mouth.

When they had finished cleaning up, she said, "Well, I thank you. Now you'd best get some rest. Farm chores start early."

"Oh, right. Good night, then."

"Good night." He wondered whether he should kiss her, but she turned away.

Jonathan went to his room and put on the nightshirt Pa had given him. He stood by the open window beside the flypaper, looking out at the dimming day. The house grew quiet. Outside, the barn and trees disappeared in mist and darkness.

A mosquito whined around Jonathan's head. He struck at it futilely, feeling more lonely by the minute.

He had never had a room to himself before. He was used to hearing carriages passing over the cobblestoned streets of New York, horses clip-clopping, music from a saloon, revelers singing, the muted laughter and voices of other orphans in Mr. Cassidy's cellar. He remembered hearing Binch Brickett hawking a late paper, and Kyle Foss shouting, "What has four legs, but only one foot? That's right! A bed!"

Now all he could hear was insects and birds. They sounded dismal out there in the foggy dark. He wondered if the dead girl, Sarah Ellen, had listened to them, too.

The thought made him shiver. He needed air. Quickly he climbed out the window and headed for the outhouse in back, his bare feet drenched in moist grass. He recalled that the path to the outhouse was lined with big blooming pink bushes—oleanders, Pa had called them. He smelled them, mist-shrouded, sweet in the dark. He followed the path between them. A damp branch brushed his cheek.

Suddenly a small ghostly white form took shape on the path before him. With a chill of horror, the words on Sarah Ellen's embroidered gravestone came into his mind: *The trumpet shall sound, and the dead shall be raised.* He gave a startled exclamation; so did the misty shape.

It was Eugenie. She was wearing a nightgown. "You scared me!" she exclaimed.

Jonathan mumbled, "I'm sorry. Excuse me." He went to the outhouse. When he returned, she was still on the path, waiting for him.

"I'm lonesome," she whispered. "I don't like it here."

"It's only our first night. We must get used to it."

"I don't like the Tildens. They're old, and they don't laugh much."

"You don't laugh much yourself. Anyway, how do

you know what they do? You slept in the wagon the whole way."

"I did not. Some of the time I was only pretending. I heard how we're supposed to call them Ma and Pa." She began to cry. "I want to be with my sister."

Jonathan didn't know what to say. The scent of oleanders was heavy in the moist air. "It's nice here right now," he offered awkwardly.

She sniffled. "At least it's fun being out at night," she admitted. "Marguerite and I were in an orphanage where you almost never went out at night."

"And I suppose other things will be fun, as we go along." Jonathan was beginning to cheer himself up, as well as her. "Maybe we'll enjoy our chores—"

He broke off as twigs crackled nearby.

A whispery voice came through the fog: "Extry! Extry!" It was the unmistakable tone of a New York City newsboy.

Jonathan could scarcely believe what he was hearing. The words were repeated: "Extry! Extry!"

There was no doubt about it. "Binch!" Jonathan exclaimed. "Binch Brickett!"

·{ **7** }··

This way," the voice hissed from the other side of a thick oleander bush.

Jonathan and Eugenie pushed past the damp branches. A lantern bobbed toward them, lighting Binch's scoop-cheeked face.

"I'm glad you're outside." His whisper was hoarse with relief. "I thought I'd have to go around tapping on windows."

"But—but—how—" Jonathan spluttered. "Where did you come from?"

"From the big white house with the pillars. You passed it when you arrived here. It's just up the road." Binch's satisfaction was evident.

"What, the landowner's house?" Jonathan asked.

"That's right. So, after all, we ended up together," Binch said smugly, "except I was adopted by a wealthy landowner, and you were adopted by a poor tenant farmer."

"What happened to my sister?" Eugenie asked.

"And Kyle Foss?" Jonathan asked eagerly.

"I don't know. When I was chosen, they hadn't

47

been taken yet. Only Big Roy Shafer was picked ahead of me. A man from New Orleans took him to a café called the Scaly Minnow." He snickered. "Right after that, I was adopted by a wealthy—"

"Oh, shut up," Eugenie said crossly. "Just go on back to your big farm, if it's so wonderful there." She flounced off toward her room.

Binch bragged to Jonathan, "I'm sure I can find Kyle, though."

"Find him? How?"

"Well, New Orleans is right on the Mississippi River. It's a big port and we're just an hour or two away from there. In fact Mr. Ashley—that's the landowner's name—"

"Get on with it. What's your plan?"

"Mr. Ashley has business in New Orleans, at one of the warehouses near the river. He's taking me with him tomorrow. I'm going to try to get down to the docks."

Jonathan began to understand. "Where the boats are."

"That's right. And if Kyle's working on one of them—"

"You might see him!" Jonathan exclaimed.

"At least I could ask around—"

Snoop around was more like it, Jonathan knew, but

for once he was thrilled by Binch's habit of gathering news. "That's wonderful!"

Binch nodded, his face conspiratorial in the lantern light. "If I can sneak out again, I'll meet you tomorrow night and let you know what I found out. Don't tell anybody, though. The Ashleys gave me a big lecture about not wandering around at night." He sounded aggrieved. "Somehow they don't trust me."

"Where shall we meet?"

"There's an old treehouse beyond the orchard, between our two houses."

"Good! After dark tomorrow, then!"

The next day Ma woke Jonathan before dawn. She gave him a pair of clean overalls. "Church ladies sent some clothes over. Hope they fit. Cows have to be milked before breakfast."

The overalls felt cool and comfortable. Jonathan dressed and went outside before he was properly awake, stumbling through the dew-soaked grass to the barn. An earthy animal smell mingled with the nose-tingling scent of hay. Pa came in with a lantern, and showed him how to grasp a cow's udder and force the milk out into the pail.

Once Jonathan got the knack of it, it wasn't hard, but it was tedious. He sat on a milking stool, moving from one large creature to another. Flies hummed around his sleepy head.

He yawned and leaned, nodding, against a cow's side. Its skin twitched, startling him. He sat up again, pulled his wits about him, and worked diligently until the job was done.

Carrying a couple of full pails across the yard to the farm cellar, as Pa had instructed him, he saw Eugenie scattering cracked corn for the chickens. They flapped down from the peach trees beside the barn where they roosted, and pecked at the feed, squabbling among themselves.

Jonathan paused for a minute, watching. The sun, a line of light, spread along the horizon. It spilled like rolling gold across the fields, glowing behind Eugenie. She wore a blue cotton dress with puffed sleeves, and a white apron. Her brown braids were tied with blue ribbons on the ends. Already she had lost the orphan look of the day before, when she had stood on the platform with wrinkled stockings and a sagging hem.

She frowned down intently at the feeding birds, scattering the corn in cautious little fans. Every gesture showed that she was anxious to do the job right.

Watching her, Jonathan smiled. He stood for long minutes, heedless of the heavy pails he was holding, until Ma strode out of the kitchen.

"Jonathan, liven up!" she called in exasperation.

"Both you younguns, get those chores done and get in here for breakfast!"

Again Millard joined them at the table, and the meal was worth working for—salt pork fried with cornmeal mush and fresh eggs, and large tin mugs of rich milk.

Obviously Ma was not going to put up with much "bashfulness" from Eugenie today. She told her briskly, "It's bakin' day, Eugenie. Hurry with the dishes, we've got a pile of work ahead of us."

Millard and Pa and Jonathan set out for the fields, leaving their lunch pails in a shady spot beside the creek. Then Millard taught Jonathan to chop and hoe young cotton plants. It looked easy when the field hand did it, but Jonathan discovered that every whack with the hoe wrenched his tight muscles. Within an hour, his hands were blistered, his back and shoulders aching.

When the sun was directly overhead, Pa called him, "Jonathan! Come eat!"

Jonathan threw down the hated hoe. Wiping his sweaty face on his sweat-streaked arm, he joined Pa and Millard beside Meander Creek. They drank from the running stream, and ate biscuits and smoked squirrel meat from their lunch pails.

"Take a rest, boy," Millard murmured to him. "We always let the noon sun pass over. Got no call to rush."

Jonathan nodded thankfully, and stretched out on the grass. He was shaded by a tree in full bloom. Its fragrance sweetened the air. Bees buzzed among its blossoms, and a redbird perched in the topmost branch, singing. Pa told him the tree's leaves would turn a fine yellow in November. He pointed out a bird's nest in a low branch.

After half an hour, they returned to the hoeing. To Jonathan, the afternoon's work seemed nearly endless. At last a cooler breeze blew over the fields. The shadows of the young corn grew long.

Millard told him, "Quittin' time," and added, "You put in a good day."

Jonathan had not been sure how well he was doing, or even if he would actually survive till nightfall. He felt a sudden lift of contentment. The day's work was done, and soon he would meet Binch. Walking back to the house, he noticed a kitten playing under a peach tree, and a young deer browsing near the pines.

He paused beside the barn to watch Barney. The dog was walking on a moving treadmill. Millard explained how the tread turned a wheel, and the wheel churned butter. He stopped the tread. "You can quit now, Barney."

The dog rolled his eyes gratefully and made a beeline for the pond. Jonathan followed, pulling off his tight boots. He let out a whoop, scaring away the long-legged birds. This time the cool water felt so good, he didn't even mind the mud.

In the kitchen, Eugenie greeted him importantly with, "Don't touch anything."

One of her brown braids was dusted with flour, and her apron was smeared with berry stains. She had baked little strawberry grunts from leftover pie filling and scraps of dough.

"We're having them for dessert," she announced, bustling and proud.

Jonathan ate heartily, then escaped to his room. Just after dark, he climbed out his window and ran through the peach trees.

Binch had said the treehouse was beyond the orchard, between the landowner's house and the Tildens'. He headed in that direction.

There was a moon, and not much mist. Twin greenish globes of animal eyes glowed among the trees. The sounds of insects rang from the fields. As he got nearer the creek, he heard a rhythmic chorus of frogs.

Beyond the last line of peaches, there was a huge live oak, trailing long curtains of moss. The moon behind it outlined a boxy shape, and Jonathan heard Binch's loud whisper: "Extry! Get your news here!"

Jonathan looked up at the flimsy structure, and saw Binch grinning at him, an odd arboreal figure in the moonlight.

"Why don't you come down?" Jonathan asked him impatiently. "Nobody's around. I don't want to climb up to that fool thing."

"Somebody might come," Binch insisted. "Besides, it's grand up here. There's a breeze and a view."

Jonathan thought the treehouse childish, if not downright dangerous. But he knew there was no arguing with Binch when he set his mind to something. He grasped the rough bark with his blistered hands, and pulled himself up. Luckily the platform of the house was not very high.

When they were both inside, Binch said, "This belonged to the Tildens' dead daughter. I guess it's ours now."

Sitting uncomfortably with his legs in the air, Jonathan snorted, "Lucky us. Now, what's the news?"

Binch started to describe the sights of New Orleans.

Jonathan cut him off impatiently. "What about Kyle? Did you find him?"

Binch shook his head. He admitted, "There must be a million boats on that river. I kept asking if they knew of a red-headed orphan boy, new on a boat. But I couldn't get a single lead."

Jonathan was stunned. He had talked himself into believing the search was bound to succeed.

"But New Orleans is a wonderful city," Binch went

on. "Mr. Ashley told me there's a place called Rue Bourbon where they make music all night long!"

"What do I care?" Jonathan mumbled.

"At least I saw Big Roy Shafer at the Scaly Minnow. The café is right near the river. We had lunch there."

With a slight rise of interest, Jonathan asked, "Roy works in the café?"

"Yes, he mops floors and does dishes and such like," Binch reported. "Seems the wrong job for him, doesn't it?"

"It does." Roy loved the outdoors. In New York, he had slept in Central Park, even when it was raining. He was a good trash picker. No bit of blowing paper escaped his eye, or his sharp trash stick.

"He's going to try to visit us one day." Binch ended, "Anyway, he doesn't know what happened to Kyle. Or to Eugenie's sister, either."

"So your trip came to nothing." Jonathan's lip trembled with disappointment. "Nothing at all."

"I wouldn't say that. We had a good lunch."

·⦃ **8** ⦄··

On Saturday night, Ma put a big tin tub out on the kitchen floor and filled it with steaming water she had heated on the stove. Eugenie and Jonathan took turns scrubbing up.

Then, wrapped in towels, they had to submit while Ma washed their hair with Packer's All Healing Tar Soap. ("Cures all hair and scalp diseases," the newspaper ads for Packer's guaranteed. "Pure as the pines.")

Packer's had a strong disinfectant smell. Eugenie protested, "That stuff is to kill bugs! I don't have bugs in my hair! No nits, and no cooties either!"

"Hold still or it'll get in your eyes," Ma told her unsympathetically.

Later they sat by the warm stove in clean nightclothes while Ma brushed out Eugenie's long brown hair and put it up in rags. The next morning, it had dried in sausage curls.

Every Sunday, they all went to church, Pa in a rusty black suit, Ma in her best grenadine dress and russet bonnet, Eugenie and Jonathan in their nicest clothes.

Jonathan had not attended any services since his years at the Foundling Home, when the Sisters had taken him to mass at St. Vincent's in New York. He had always enjoyed it. Now while Eugenie fidgeted and yawned through the sermon, he took in every word, thrilled by the preacher's stormy tone and long words.

He recognized the service as being, in its way, a performance. The preacher was its star. Miss Tibbitts, who played the little organ, was second in importance, while members of the congregation were both audience and chorus.

Jonathan never failed to do his part. He folded his hands and joined in the prayers. He sang the hymns lustily. When the collection plate was passed he was tempted to pinch a few coins, but refrained.

The Ashleys, plump and well-dressed, attended the same church. They sat in the front pew with Binch, a prosperous-looking trio. Binch wore a new suit, instead of hand-me-downs like Eugenie and Jonathan.

Occasionally the Tildens invited some farm family to share their Sunday noon dinner. In return, they were invited to neighboring farms.

At first these visits worried Jonathan. He was nervously quiet and polite, moved cautiously without bumping into anyone or anything, sat where he was told. He never helped himself too soon, nor took too much. He never ate potato skins. He didn't make quips or indulge in what Ma called "flighty remarks," but just listened.

Mostly the talk was about farming, the weather, the price of butter. Sometimes it was about how the Yankees had ruined the South. Though the Civil War had been over for twenty years, Louisiana was still very poor, and many of its people were bitter about the Northern victory.

Jonathan feared this might be one more thing against him: he was a stranger, an orphan, *and* a Yankee. But the neighbors treated him kindly. He felt pretty well accepted in Meander Creek, though he always had a sense of inner distraction, as if he didn't quite belong here.

After supper on Sunday evenings, the newly formed Tilden family sat together in the kitchen. Once or twice Jonathan played tunes for the others—"Amazing Grace," which Ma appreciated especially, or "Old Dog Tray," Pa's choice. They listened politely, Ma keeping time with her thimble. Both liked music, but, as Ma said, they heard it in church. Usually the family soon got on to other things.

Pa preferred to read the almanac, or the mail-order catalogues. Ma usually worked on her embroidery. She taught Eugenie the cross-stitch, and started her on a sampler.

"You pick a Bible verse and I'll trace it out for you on the linen," she told the girl.

"You know I can't read," Eugenie objected.

"Fetch your Bible here. Let's see what we can do."

Eugenie got the Bible with her name on it in gold letters. Ma opened the book and found a place. "Here's a good one. 'I cry aloud to the Lord, and he answers me from his holy hill.' "

Eugenie frowned, puzzled. "Why am I crying?"

"It means if you seek help, the Lord will help you."

"Then why doesn't it say that?"

Ma sighed, and turned more pages. "Now this would be lovely," she declared. " 'Praise the Lord from the heavens, praise him from the heights.' You could embroider stars and clouds around it."

"Too long." Eugenie set her chin stubbornly. "I don't want to sew that many words."

Ma started to argue. Eugenie's round face looked like a storm cloud.

Jonathan interjected, "How about just 'Praise the Lord'?"

"Perfect," Eugenie said promptly.

Jonathan returned to his book, an inspiring tale by Horatio Alger titled *Ragged Dick; or, Street Life in New York with the Bootblacks*. It was one of several books in a charity box the church ladies had sent over. Jonathan had never read a storybook before, and found it enthralling. He resolved to rise in the world like Ragged Dick.

On other evenings, he read "The Youth's Companion," a paper that came to him secondhand from Binch. The Ashleys had given Binch a subscription to it. Jonathan liked its accounts of death-defying tiger hunts in India and terrifying cannibal attacks in Peru.

There were self-improvement articles, too. By the end of the evening when the lamp burned low, he was dazzled by eyestrain and good intentions.

He liked Sundays, and usually fell asleep to happy thoughts. Yet his dreams were no better than during the week.

Ever since he had gotten here, he kept dreaming he was on the Orphan Train again, riding, riding, to a place he never reached.

Millard did not eat with the Tildens on Sundays. He cooked for himself and ate in his own house, or joined black friends for a meal.

He didn't go to church with the Tildens, either. Jonathan found out that the black people had their own church, the Solid Rock Gospel Ministry, about a mile away. On Tuesday evenings, they held a prayer meeting and sang gospel songs.

After Millard told him this, Jonathan followed him secretly through the moonrise of one Tuesday night, and lay on the grass outside his church, listening to the music. It had a fervent beat that made him long to jump up, clap his hands, play a haunting instrument of some kind. Much of it seemed livelier and more rousing than the hymns Jonathan sang in the white people's church.

His tin whistle lay unused in his pocket, but next day, in the fields, he pulled it out and tried to play the wonderful tunes he had heard. He became so lost in the music that he did not notice Millard coming close to listen.

Then Millard remarked, "You play 'Swing Low' mighty good, for a white boy."

Jonathan jumped, startled. He laughed guiltily. "I like it a lot."

"Where'd you learn it?"

Jonathan told him.

Millard nodded, without comment. After a minute, he said, "Play on. I didn't mean to disturb you."

That began a friendship between Millard and Jonathan. A night or two later, feeling lonely, Jonathan walked out to the field hand's cabin. The voices of insects and birds rang through the pine woods.

Millard greeted Jonathan warmly, from a chair in front of his cabin. "I'll get another chair from inside, if you aim to set a spell."

"I'll set right here." Jonathan sat on the ground. It was cushioned with pine needles. They were quiet for a while, as a big moon rose behind the pines.

At last Millard asked, "How you like it in Meander Creek so far?"

Jonathan hesitated. The question took him unaware. "The food is good. And the work seems easier than it did at the beginning. I like—well, Sundays—"

"Sounds like there's a *but* comin' up."

"But—I think of a plan I made with a friend." He told him about Kyle, and about Binch's trip to New Orleans. "I know it's dumb, but I'd like to go to the Mississippi River and try to find Kyle for myself."

"Nothin' dumb about that."

"Yes, there is. He could be anywhere. And the Tildens are kind to me. I'm lucky."

"Well, you're right about the Tildens. They're sensible people. No other white folk ever asked me to set down at the table with 'em for meals. Miz Tilden says since they freed the slaves, she reckons we're as good as anybody else." He chuckled. "Sounds like we was poison before, but she means well."

"Orphans are poison to some people, too," Jonathan said, remembering the insults in Laitue.

"I reckon."

Millard was pretty close to an orphan himself. He had been born into slavery, and his parents had been sold to a distant plantation when he was a baby. When he was twelve years old, the Civil War had ended and he was freed.

"I hopped on a boxcar and rode the rails. Didn't know where I was goin', but I wanted a life that belonged to me. *My own life.*"

Jonathan was struck by these words. When he had boarded the Orphan Train, he had felt exactly the same. He still did. He always had the sense of pulling away from Meander Creek.

"I was one happy boy when I rode that train. See, freedom don't get you a job, and it don't get you a home," Millard amplified. "But it do give you *possibilities.*"

The word echoed inside Jonathan. Even now he felt that anything was possible.

He asked Millard, "How'd you get by?"

"Well, I wandered," the field hand answered. "If I could get a job in a kitchen someplace, I took that. If I could wash dishes in a restaurant, I just did it. And I worked seasonal."

"Seasonal?"

"When the cotton comes in, you pick cotton. Or say it's early spring, you pick strawberries. Then there's yams, and okra. You got plantin' time and pickin' time, so you move on to wherever they need you. Trapped muskrats and otters. Caught catfish and bullfrogs. There's a good market in bullfrogs."

"I heard they serve frogs' legs in fancy restaurants in New York. I never was in one, though."

"They serve 'em in New Orleans, too," Millard said. "What about you? How'd you get along in New York City, on your own?"

Jonathan told him.

Millard nodded. "Street performing's a good way. In New Orleans, a lot of freed slaves do that for a living. They dance the rag, and throw in a swing and a stomp, and they're makin' a whole new kind of music. Folks call it ragtime."

"Wish I could hear it."

"It's mighty lively. Couple of years back, a friend of mine give me his banjo. He got a hotel job, and quit playin'. I thought I might go into street music myself, but I couldn't get the knack of it."

"So do you want to stay here always? Is this what you were looking for?"

Millard shook his head. "There's a new railroad,

linkin' up New Orleans with the West Coast—the Southern Pacific. I'd like to get me a job on that railroad. That's what I want."

They looked up at the moon as it sailed above the pines. They were lost in their own dreams.

Jonathan asked, "What did you do with that old banjo?"

"Got it inside." Millard went into his cabin and brought the instrument out. He handed it to Jonathan, who had never held one before, though he had often listened to them on the streets of New York.

Jonathan cradled it clumsily. It had a broken string that dangled over its side. He plucked one of the whole strings, then another. They had a dull muzzy sound, not the way they should be.

"How do you tune it?" he asked.

"You tighten them pegs." Millard showed him. "Strings are pretty old, though. They may not hold the pitch too good."

Jonathan could tell the notes weren't exactly right, but they enchanted him. He tried to strum "Little Brown Jug." He couldn't quite get it, because of the broken string and the fact that the others kept slipping lower in pitch, but still—

He plunked and plunked, imagining a fine melodic twang.

Finally Millard burst out laughing. "Reckon that old banjo should belong to you!"

Jonathan looked up, his face radiant. "You mean it?"

"Sure do. Seems to me you got the makin's of a banjo player."

·⟨ 9 ⟩·

Jonathan was out by the pond after supper, practicing his banjo.

Eugenie came out. "Can I listen?"

"All right." He twanged through a piece, pretending the instrument had a fine strong ring. "How does it sound?"

"Bad."

"Oh, thank you very much, Eugenie."

"You asked me."

He snapped, "What do you expect? It's not just my playing, it's the strings!"

"You *asked* me."

He checked his anger, and grinned ruefully. "Doesn't mean I wanted you to tell me."

A week later, Jonathan was beginning his days' work in the fields when he saw a husky figure striding along the road.

With pleasure and surprise, he shouted, "Roy! Big Roy!" He threw down his hoe and ran to greet his old friend.

Roy clapped him on the arm and explained that he had walked the seven or eight miles from New Orleans. The owner of the Scaly Minnow had given him a day off.

"I stopped by and ate with Binch and his new family." Roy grinned. "He struck it rich, didn't he?"

"Yes. We eat good here, too," Jonathan said. "How about you? Working in a café, I guess you're not starving, either."

"No, I can't complain about that." Roy shaded his eyes, and looked over the sun-shimmered fields. "But I'd give a lot to work outdoors, like you do. This is a dandy place."

Jonathan joked, "You want to help with the hoeing, you'll be welcome. Right, Millard?"

"Anytime," the field hand assured him. "Just fetch a hoe from the shed."

Roy took them up on it. He threw his husky body into the task. By afternoon, he had accomplished so much that Pa said they could all quit early.

When Roy had to leave to walk back to New Orleans, he told Jonathan, "That was a fine day. I enjoyed it."

"So did I," Jonathan said fervently. "Come again!"

After that, whenever Roy got a day off, he strode along the road to Meander Creek, his broad face wearing an eager smile. "Farming comes natural to me," he said with bashful pride. "Seems like I was born to it."

He kept urging Jonathan to visit him in New Orleans at the Scaly Minnow. "Mr. Nockle—he's the owner—is sure to give you a meal."

"I want to," Jonathan assured him. "I'll try."

He longed to see the city, but wasn't sure he should ask for a day off. Then one evening when he and Pa were catching crayfish in the creek, he decided to broach the subject. He began cautiously, "Pa, do you ever go into New Orleans?"

"Now and then," Pa replied. "Got no plans to go just now, though. Why?"

"I'd like to visit Roy." They were using small wire nets of cotton mesh to scoop the wriggling shellfish out of the water and dump them into a pail. A crayfish squirmed out of Jonathan's net and fell onto the sunset-dappled bank of the creek. He tried to get the wire under it, but it scuttled into the water again. He and Pa watched it disappear in the stream.

Jonathan scooped up another netful and transferred them quickly to the pail. "Roy asked me to come."

"Well, I got no plans right now," Pa repeated.

"Could I borrow the wagon and go by myself, then?"

"We need the wagon here on the farm."

"If you could spare me for a whole day, I could walk."

"Someday, maybe. . . . Watch that little critter, he's gettin' away from you!"

Someday . . .

But there was always so much to do. Jonathan had to strip suckers from the tobacco plants, build a henhouse, weed the okra, hoe the yams and cotton, help Ma make butter. He had to learn to fish and hunt.

Before coming to Meander Creek, he had never held a gun. He was a poor shot, partly because he didn't like hearing the small shriek of a dying animal or seeing birds fall out of the sky. It ruined his aim to think of these things.

But he saw an alligator kill a baby coon in a single snap, saw a lively fish leap in the air to catch a bug, watched a hawk swoop down on a mouse. He began to understand that killing meant food. Gradually his aim improved.

Sometimes he shot and skinned blackbirds. Ma dipped the birds in cornmeal and cooked them in butter. Eugenie learned to make a good blackbird pie, using carrots and onions from the kitchen garden.

Jonathan was glad some birds didn't make good eating. He admired the fierce-eyed herons that fished in the creek. He enjoyed the peeping songs of chickadees, and felt a rush of elation when red-tailed hawks flew by.

In June the tobacco crop was harvested. Jonathan and Millard cut the stalks with a cane knife, then hung them in the drying shed, safe from sun and from the seasonal rains that soaked the fields.

During this wet weather, the downpours often stopped after supper. Huge gilt-rimmed clouds would move across the western sky. A fresh smell of mud rose from the earth, and grasses glittered.

In the steamy air of long summer evenings, Jonathan and Pa took their fishing poles to the creek. They caught catfish and mullet, and soft-shelled cooter turtles that Ma fried like rabbit.

Hot weather brought an abundance of alligators and poisonous snakes to the banks of streams. Jonathan learned that a log, seen close up, might be a 'gator. Snakes masqueraded as vines or fallen branches.

"Wild critters don't want to meet up with us. They'll get away before we even see 'em, if they can," Millard told him. "But if you startle a cottonmouth or a 'gator, and you get too close, they can move mighty fast—and mighty mean."

Jonathan was careful. When Pa taught him and Binch to swim in a sinkhole rimmed by pines, he was scared of every moving ripple, mistaking it for a cotton-mouth. He had occasional shivers of horror, hearing the shriek of a wildcat in the night.

Once, seeing a bear startlingly near among the berry bushes, he felt his heart pounding like a drum. But the big animal crashed away, as scared as he was.

After this encounter, he sat down on a rock, shaken. Spring and early summer had passed, and still no one on the Tilden farm had been to New Orleans.

That night, his usual train dream was a nightmare. As he rode on and on, the train filled with snakes and 'gators, and a bear sat beside him, asking, "Why did you choose this seat?"

He began to realize he didn't like Meander Creek, and maybe never would.

Jonathan played his whistle in the fields, he hummed, he could hardly wait for Sunday and the hymns. Tuesday evenings he lay on the cool grass outside Millard's church and listened to the gospel songs.

And he tried—oh, how he tried—to play the banjo. He imagined how the missing string might sound; how the others would sound, too, if they were tuned right.

"Can I listen?" Eugenie asked.

"No," he told her rudely.

O_n the Fourth of July, there was a church picnic. All the ladies brought covered baskets of fried chicken and smoked fish, corn bread, fancy cakes and pies. Long tables were set up near the graveyard.

"You're mighty welcome to share with us," families told each other, opening up the baskets.

Methods were discussed, recipes exchanged. Ma had brought a ten-egg cake, proof that Make-Um-Lay Poultry Powder, which she had mixed in the chicken feed, was every bit as good as advertised. "Mr. Tilden ordered it from Ward's," she explained.

"Oh, you can rely on Ward's." Mrs. Ashley nodded vivaciously. "They keep up to date." She advised Mrs. Deland, whose daughter was notably pasty-faced, "You should try the new Dr. Williams' Pink Pills for Pale People on your Lucie Marie. Perk her right up!"

"That so?"

"I should say! It's a wonder! Why, you-all recall how yellow my Binch used to look. Well, I just made him take Dr. Williams', and see now!"

Sure enough, Binch's sallow skin had turned quite rosy. He smirked, glad to be the center of attention.

"We use Carter's Little Liver Pills," young Mrs. Grenier put in shyly.

"I declare, I don't know *what* to try," Mrs. Deland sighed.

Her pallid daughter squirmed away and asked Eugenie, "Want some gum?"

"I don't mind." Eugenie helped herself from the package of Adams' Black Jack Chewing Gum. She had never tasted flavored gum before. Captivated by the licorice taste, she swallowed four sticks before anybody could stop her.

"Will they lodge in her liver?" Ma asked, alarmed.

Mrs. Grenier reckoned a dose of Carter's might be a wise precaution.

Eugenie crossed her eyes, pretended to retch, and scampered off.

Pa and some other men drew straws, and formed teams for horseshoes. Jonathan joined the boys in games of snap-the-whip and mumblety-peg.

Later he entered a contest to keep a wooden top spinning on an overturned gravestone. He won, and was given a prize, a handsome cat's-eye marble.

He had a fine time, until the sun went down. Then he realized the holiday was almost over. Shadows stretched blue and gloomy in the graveyard. Its ancient trees and hanging moss seemed swept by a melancholy wind.

Jonathan sat alone on the slab where he and the others had spun the tops. He looked over the graves. Young men who had fought in the war lay here, brought back from the battlefields where they had died. Children lay here, dead of cholera and yellow fever.

He thought of the Tildens' daughter, forever five years old, waiting for the trumpet to sound.

Young women had died in childbirth. Old people had just died. Everyone met here. Everything ended here.

A mockingbird perched on a gravestone and sang in the deepening dusk. Its song seemed terribly sad, the liquid notes dipping down. Suddenly Jonathan felt like weeping. Life seemed so hard, so futile.

In the darkness, grown-ups chatted quietly. A few children played hide-and-seek. Fireflies floated up like sparks from the misty grasses.

Then, as the stars appeared, a fiddler began to play, sawing out the melodies of "The Old Oaken Bucket," "In the Sweet By and By," "The Little Brown Church in the Vale."

Gradually Jonathan's heavy spirits lifted. When the fiddler took a break, he stepped up and piped a few tunes on his whistle. He chose happy songs, rollicking songs.

Some of the older people had gone home, but younger ones clapped their hands and sang. Lantern light flickered over them. Their faces seemed to glow with joy and fun, as if the music filled them with a rare shining energy.

Jonathan paused to draw breath and to gulp lemonade. "I wish we could do this all the time!" he burst out to Binch.

"Do what?"

"Oh—make music! Sing! Live on the top of things!" he stammered.

Binch squinted at him, puzzled.

·{ **10** }··

By late summer, the Tildens' fall crops were thriving. There was not so much field work to be done, but fences had to be mended, wood cut and stored, a shutter replaced on the farmhouse.

Jonathan often helped Ma make butter, a long process. The fresh milk had to be strained through racks into tin pans, where it "set" until the cream had risen to the top. Then the cream was skimmed and saved until there was enough for a churning. Barney, on his dog tread, did the hard work of operating the churn.

Jonathan watched as the butter came, the cream turning miraculously to thick fatty gold. He scooped it out of the churn into a large butter bowl, then pushed it back and forth with a ladle to get the buttermilk out. Nothing was wasted: the skimmed milk was made into cottage cheese. The buttermilk was stored in crocks, to drink or use in baking. Eugenie made a horrible face when she drank it, but Jonathan thought it delicious.

Finally the butter itself, with salt added by Ma, was packed into tubs to be sold.

. . . .

In September, the Tildens told Jonathan that since he could read and write and do sums, he did not have to attend school. Eugenie, though, began going to the local one-room schoolhouse every weekday, except when she was especially needed at home. Usually she fed the chickens and helped clean up breakfast, then set out with her books and lunch pail. After the first few mornings, she went quite cheerfully.

To Binch's shock, he had to go, too. He complained furiously to Jonathan, "What do I need with school? I can read any newspaper, and I've been figuring change all my life!"

It was true, but Mr. Ashley insisted on formal studies for his son, so off Binch went.

After that he never missed a chance to show off his new knowledge. Passing Jonathan on the road after school, he informed him, "Parsing sentences is a true art."

Cutting across an acre where Jonathan was mulching strawberry plants with dry pine straw, he remarked, "Coloring maps isn't easy. Few people realize how many continents there are. And separate *countries*—"

"Spare me, Binch."

Next he won a spelling bee, and would have announced it to the whole state of Louisiana if he could.

During the harvest season, as Jonathan worked sweatily in the fields, he saw Binch and Eugenie walking home together, swinging their lunch pails in their hands. He had no desire to attend school, yet the sight of them gave him a bruised, left-out feeling.

He noticed how often Ma and Pa helped Eugenie with her lessons in the evening, how much they praised her clumsy embroidery. They encouraged her to play in the treehouse, when she might have been doing chores. While she perched there like a princess, Ma would report back to Pa, "She's looking at her storybook in the treehouse," or "She's eating an orange in the treehouse," always adding, "Like Sarah Ellen used to do."

Jonathan hated the treehouse. He wouldn't have wanted to eat or read in the stupid place. But Ma and Pa never commented on anything he *did* like. They never asked about his progress with the banjo, even though he had told them about it.

He could not, in fact, make much progress, with one broken string, and the others slipping out of tune. Yet in spare moments he kept plunking at it, and Millard was the only person who took an interest. Except Eugenie, of course, and she didn't count.

"Someday it'll be different," Jonathan told himself, when his moods of sadness and discontent seemed unbearable. But he had no idea when or how.

. . . .

At the Foundling Home, the Sisters had celebrated a birthday for each child, whether they knew the real birth date or not. Jonathan's was October fifth. He always felt sad early in October, knowing he would not have the present or the small cake the Sisters would have given him.

In Meander Creek, when the last of the leaves fell from the catalpa trees and the nights grew cool, his seasonal gloom returned.

On October fourth, he and Ma made butter. Tomorrow was his thirteenth birthday. It should be a special day. But like Christmas when he was homeless and Thanksgiving when he was hungry, he knew it would just be a reminder of the lacks in his life.

Flies buzzed around the butter tubs as they packed them. When they had finished the lot, Ma asked, "How'd you like to go with Millard to the market tomorrow?"

"All right."

As though it were of no consequence, Ma added, "He has an errand in New Orleans, so he'll sell this batch at the city market."

For a moment, Jonathan didn't take in the meaning of this. Then he gasped, "New Orleans? I'm—I'm going to *New Orleans* tomorrow?"

Only the glint in Ma's eyes showed she was pleased by his reaction. "The French Market there pays better for butter than we can get around here. Not worth goin' that long way, though, unless there's another errand to be done."

"Oh, we'll do the errand! That is, Millard will. We *both* will. That is—" Jonathan was incoherent at the prospect of the trip. "Thank you!" he babbled. "Thank you!"

"Huh," Ma sniffed. But she gave him her thin smile.

Next morning Jonathan and Millard loaded the butter tubs in the wagon and left home before dawn. They reached New Orleans just as the city's bustle was beginning.

Giddy with expectation, Jonathan gaped at the crowds, the fancy shops and restaurants. During his months in Meander Creek, he had grown used to seeing plain farmhouses and barns, with more cows and chickens than people.

Here the narrow streets and raised wooden sidewalks were crowded, the morning din a cacophany of voices, and clopping horses, and jangling bicycle bells. Many of the buildings had courtyards, and wrought-iron balconies spilling with flowers.

"Creole style," Millard explained. "French and Spanish folks settled in New Orleans and built like what they were used to."

From behind a fan-shaped window, Jonathan heard music, lively as the morning. *Music!*

"I like this!" he exclaimed. "I like it here!"

Millard promised, "After we get our butter sold, we'll ride around some. See the sights."

"Can we go to the river?" Jonathan asked eagerly.

"Sure thing. And lookee here—" They reached the corner of Rampart and Rue Orleans. "Slaves used to meet here on Sundays to dance and play music—African drums, handmade instruments, like that. It was called Congo Square. And across here, on Rue Bourbon, you can see street performers most any night."

They jogged on with their load. At a crossroad, a young boy in a varnished yellow pony cart veered close to the wagon. Millard pulled sharply on the reins, checking the old farm horse before they could collide. The boy, cocky in his jaunty wagon and fine clothes, gave a negligent wave and passed by. He glanced at Jonathan as though he were no more than a post in the road.

Jonathan's pride and anger stirred. He was suddenly aware of the faded, tattered overalls he was wearing, the wide straw hat. He looked like a poor country boy, unworthy of attention.

"Well, I'm not," he mumbled aloud, glaring after the pony cart. "Not really."

"What?" Millard asked.

Jonathan shrugged, his jaw set.

As they got nearer the French Market, the streets grew even more crowded. Wagons and pushcart peddlers competed for space. Farm women pushed through the throngs, carrying ducks and chickens and baskets of eggs. Street vendors cried, "Buy my pralines! Buy my fresh fish!" Some hawked in accented phrases, "*Beignets! Café au lait!*"

Wagons loaded with larger wares, like Ma's butter tubs, turned off into separate streets where their products were bought in bulk.

Jonathan watched as the butter buyer lined up the tubs, then pushed a rod down into the middle of each one, and licked the butter off. After each lick, he wiped the rod with a dirty rag, and sampled another tub. The procedure surprised Jonathan. In Meander Creek, the buyer always took the Tildens' wares on faith, knowing their milk was rich and flavorful and the product good. He just counted the tubs, glanced in to be sure they were full, and bought them, chatting and passing the time of day with Millard all the while.

But obviously competition was keener here in the city, and Millard was quiet and tense through the sampling. Jonathan wondered if it might turn out that Ma's butter wasn't up to standard. Suppose the lot was rejected, and they had to go home with all these tubs unsold?

After the last lick, the buyer nodded and made Millard an offer. It was higher than any amount they had ever been offered in Meander Creek. Jonathan felt like cheering, but knew that was no way to bargain. He remained grave. Millard merely gave an answering nod. The tubs were unloaded. Money changed hands.

"Move on." The buyer waved them along. The farm horse pulled the lightened wagon easily, though slowly, through the crowded streets.

To Jonathan, the episode seemed to sum up the solid advantages of city living. If you did well, met higher standards, your reward might be greater than you dreamed. He felt he had learned a valuable lesson.

·{ **11** }··

They clopped on past Jackson Square and the old cathedral. Jonathan paid little attention as Millard pointed these out. Then they turned a corner onto a street where the crowds were thinner, the view clearer. Jonathan caught a glimpse of sparkling water.

"The river!" he shouted.

"The river," Millard agreed with a grin.

He hitched the horse at the curb. Jonathan jumped down from the seat and ran, almost flew, past salt warehouses to the levee. As he climbed up its bank, he could smell the rich dank river smell. He heard toots and whistles and clanging bells. From on top, he looked down on the broad, shining Mississippi.

Its brown water was busy with stern-wheelers and shanty boats, side-wheelers, tugs, barges. The docks swarmed with black workers loading baled freight, heaving crates and boxes, tugging ropes, cleaning fish, shouting to each other.

Finely dressed passengers stepped off a packet boat. One gentleman, immaculate in spotless gray, waved away a ragged bootblack as though the boy were a bothersome fly.

Jonathan admired the gentleman's clothes, his cool disdain. He was thrilled by the immensity and contrasts of this river world.

Above the restless water, gulls flew white against the blue sky, catching fish guts tossed from a fishing boat. They swooped and soared.

Jonathan took off his hat to feel the river wind. It blew back his straight dark hair, stung his tanned skin, seemed to carry him right up to the clouds. He felt as high and light as the birds.

He would have stood all day, all night, maybe forever. But Millard reminded him, "I still got an errand to do, and you might like to stop by the Scaly Minnow. See Roy."

"Yes. Yes, I would."

They found the little café without much trouble. Millard stopped at the door and said, "You go on in. I'll come back in 'bout half an hour. Wait for me outside."

Jonathan nodded, and went in. The café had just a few tables, each one lavishly supplied with the usual free bread and piccalilli. Signs on a wall suggested, *Try Our Gumbo, Big Bowl 10¢. 2 Sinkers and Coffee 5¢. Chew the Best Tobacco. We Sell Honest Scrap.* Next to this was the customary reminder, *No Spitting.*

86

Jonathan spotted Roy right away. He was serving a customer. When he saw Jonathan, a smile lit his wide face. He hurried forward, wiping his hands on his apron.

A short, stocky red-headed man came out of the kitchen and smiled quizzically at Jonathan, who recognized him at once. It was the man who had teased Kyle about having the same color hair as his own.

"I know you, don't I?" the man asked now.

Jonathan whipped off his hat. "Yes, sir. I was one of the orphans in Laitue. Jonathan Dale."

"Ah, yes. Roy visits you sometimes in Meander Creek."

"That's right, sir. We're always very pleased to see him."

The man nodded, his face good-humored. "Well, I suspect he's always glad to go." Roy blushed and turned away. He cleared a table hastily, dropping a spoon, spilling some leftover coffee.

"What, glad to get away from the Scaly Minnow?" a customer joked. "Why, I'd spend all my time here, if the missus'd let me."

Everybody laughed except Roy, who was earnestly wiping up the spilled coffee. Jonathan noticed that although he was so strong and capable on the farm, Roy seemed clumsy here. He clattered off to the kitchen with used dishes.

The red-headed man jabbed his own chest with his thumb. "Meet Brett Nockle, owner of the Scaly Minnow. And my missus." He indicated an aproned young lady with a sharp, pretty face. She nodded.

"Sit down, lad. Have a bowl of gumbo," Mr. Nockle went on.

"I'm afraid I don't have time, sir."

Another customer spoke up. "You're missing a treat, son. The best tomatoes and okras beg to be picked for the Minnow's gumbo!"

Jonathan ventured a quick joke of his own: "I know. I live on a farm, and I've heard them begging."

Mr. Nockle slapped him cordially on the shoulder and joined in the general laughter.

A customer held out a mug. "Where's Roy gone? I want some more coffee."

"That Roy. Always in the wrong place at the wrong time." Mrs. Nockle tossed her head, frowning.

"I'll get it," Jonathan offered, and hurried into the kitchen. Roy was doing dishes, his brawny arms elbow-deep in dishwater.

Jonathan filled the coffee cup from a tall pot on the stove. The act of pouring the steaming brew gave him a warm, unaccustomed feeling of hospitality. "It's nice here," he said happily.

Roy looked at him, puzzled. "You think so?"

"I do. Friendly people, easy work."

Roy nodded slowly. "Maybe we should trade jobs."

Jonathan laughed. "Maybe." He hurried back to the customers.

At home that evening, Jonathan washed up quickly and joined the others for supper. He realized at once that something odd was going on. Pa and Ma exchanged darting looks, Eugenie gave a stifled giggle. Millard wore an expression of false nonchalance, his mouth curving irresistibly upward.

They were all standing around the kitchen table as though waiting for company.

Bewildered, Jonathan asked, "What's happening?"

"Somebody's a year older," Ma replied, pulling her face into a mysterious pout.

Pa brought a wrapped package from behind his back. "Happy birthday from Ma and me."

Jonathan took the package, hardly believing it was really for him. No one had mentioned his birthday until this moment. He had almost forgotten about it himself.

He tore off the brown wrapping. Inside was a pair of brand-new Levi's Patent Riveted 501 Waist High Overalls, with the famous two-horse guarantee patch in back. The overalls were in his size.

Levi's, the sturdiest workpants going, and with *rivets!* Jonathan touched the leather back patch, too overcome to speak. This was the first garment he had ever owned that was not a hand-me-down.

"Ma—Pa—I—I—" he stammered.

"Good," Ma said briskly, as though he had managed to express himself. "Now, Eugenie, you next."

Eugenie brought forward a roll of cloth tied with a ribbon. "Happy birthday."

He unrolled the stiff buckram. It was an embroidered room tidy. Each pocket had been sewn on with a different color thread, giving a pretty effect. He could tell from the erratic stitches that the tidy was Eugenie's own work, and that it had cost her considerable effort.

"It's for keeping things in. You're supposed to hang it on the wall," she told him.

"I know. I will. I've needed a keeping place. I'll put my marbles in it, and my comb and my whistle—" He imagined his small possessions safely tucked in the pockets. The vision gave him a rare sense of order and stability.

"Well, I—" He tried to pull his wits together to make a general speech of thanks. "I surely am—well, amazed, and—"

"We're not through yet," Millard interrupted, his dark eyes warm and smiling. "I bought you somethin' in New Orleans. It don't look like much, but maybe you'll like it." He slipped an envelope into Jonathan's hand.

Jonathan opened the envelope. At first he didn't realize what the five coiled strings in the envelope were for. Then he realized they were new banjo strings.

His face flooded with astonished joy. Without a word, he pushed back his chair to get the banjo.

Ma stopped him. "You sit right in your place, young man. I made a honey cake."

He sank down, grinning. "How did you know it was my birthday?"

"It was in the papers the Children's Aid Society gave us," Pa told him. "Your 'presumed date of birth.' "

Jonathan wondered if the papers were for his final adoption by the Tildens. It was a subject he didn't want to bring up.

"Honey cake," he said hurriedly. "My favorite."

·{ **12** }··

Once he got the new strings on, Jonathan's banjo seemed to come alive in his hands. Tunes sprang out of it, and chords, and the fast hard rhythms he loved. He knew his playing was faulty, heard that his harmonies were simple and sometimes downright bad.

Yet he was learning, and he grudged the field work that kept him from practicing as much as he wanted to.

It was cotton-picking time. Each day's labor was long and hard.

With seven-foot cloth sacks looped over their shoulders and dragging behind them, he and Pa and Millard moved along the rows, plucking the cotton from the tough brown bolls. Jonathan's hands were strong and calloused now, yet the bolls cut his skin, his back ached to breaking, and his big straw hat slipped with sweat.

Poisonous snakes were common in the fields. He learned to keep alert for the rattlers' warning whirr and the cottonmouths' musky smell. When either was detected, Millard killed the snake if he could.

"Once a farm dog died right beside me from a

cottonmouth bite," he told Jonathan, who began imagining the dreaded musky smell every time he drew breath.

All day Jonathan looked forward to evening, when the miserable hot hours in the field would be over and he could practice again. Eugenie did her schoolwork at the kitchen table after supper. If Ma and Pa were not too busy with their own chores, they smiled and listened as she read aloud from her McGuffey's Reader.

"Ax," she read, looking at the pictures and the words alongside. "Box. Cat. Dog. Elk."

Jonathan knew his banjo could be heard through the thin walls. To avoid disturbing her, he usually took the instrument outside to practice.

One evening, after he had been picking cotton since sunup, he slogged wearily with the banjo to the edge of the pond. He sank down on the cool soft bank, discouraged and exhausted. He wanted to work on "Turkey in the Straw," and finally began, but the first stroke of his cut fingers across the strings made him cry out with pain.

A sudden desperation washed over him. He held the banjo against his chest, his head bent, eyes squeezed shut. The blue evening seemed to close around him. Empty time went by, and it struck him that this was to be his life.

He heard the distant voices of wild geese flying

overhead. They were moving south from their nesting grounds in Canada to winter feeding grounds in the Louisiana marshes. All month they had filled the evening skies, following their migration route on the Mississippi Flyway. They seemed to call to Jonathan, their voices a strange inhuman summons to a wider world.

As their calls grew louder and louder, he looked up, but they were flying too high for him to see them. They clamored overhead; then the honking sounds faded as they flew on.

Jonathan thought of how far the geese had traveled, what hardships they had endured. Yet they went on.

All anyone could do was go on.

He searched on the ground and found a thin piece of wood. He plucked the banjo strings with it. It spared his fingers and gave him a louder twang. He practiced "Turkey in the Straw" until it was late and cold outside, and Ma came to find him.

Next morning when Jonathan finished the milking, Pa reminded him that he had left a hoe in the kitchen garden. "Put it in the toolshed, son. We can't be dropping tools all over the place."

Jonathan found the hoe. As he picked it up, a loud hollow buzz froze him. With a jolt of terror, he recognized the sound, and saw the rattler. It was a big one, probably four or five feet long, no more than a yard away. Its tail vibrated with the dry whirring rattle, a deadly warning. Its wedge-shaped head was held tense and high. The snake was coiled to strike.

In a wash of horror, Jonathan stepped backward. His heart thudded. He heard his own raspy breathing along with the rattler's buzz. His foot slipped. He steadied himself. The snake swayed slightly, powerful and ready.

From inside the house, Eugenie called, "Jonathan? Come on in for breakfast."

He didn't answer.

"Jonathan?"

He heard her step on the creaky kitchen floor.

At that instant, he realized he couldn't back off and leave the rattler here in the kitchen garden. He had to kill it before it bit Eugenie, or Barney, or any of them.

He just had to kill it.

He tightened his grip on the hoe. He visualized a curve between its cutting edge and a spot where the snake's body touched the ground.

He swung the hoe with all his force.

The impact jarred his wrists and shoulder. The wild rattle of the snake clattered like hail on a tin roof.

Jonathan struck again with the hoe, cleanly, near the head. The blow nearly severed it, yet the body still writhed. The snake's tail did a mad dance. But now there was no purpose in it, no power.

The snake flopped around like a vine in a stream. Jonathan knew it was done for. Wrenched by revulsion, he threw down the hoe. He backed away from the contorted body and ran into the kitchen.

"Pa—in the kitchen garden—don't go out, Eugenie—"

He lurched to the outhouse and threw up. He retched helplessly, his throat burning.

In a while, Ma called through the outhouse door, "Your breakfast's waiting, Jonathan."

"I can't eat," he gasped.

"Yes, you can. For strength. Come on."

He staggered out and followed her to the kitchen. The men had left for the cotton field. Eugenie had gone to school.

Ma rinsed Jonathan's hands and face with cool water. She gave him a drink of sugar water to soothe his sore throat. She eased him into his seat at the table, and put a plate of eggs and grits before him. There was honey on the grits, the way he liked them best. She sat down beside him with a cup of coffee.

"Eat," she murmured, and he did.

Alone with her in the quiet kitchen, he listened to

the harmless buzz of flies. The sound tightened his nerves, reminding him of the snake's rattle.

He asked faintly, "Did Pa take it away?"

"Yes."

"It's gone."

"Yes."

Jonathan said vehemently, "I'll never go into that kitchen garden again."

She replied, "You went in the garden today. You met a rattler. Now you're sittin' here eatin' honeyed grits." She sipped her coffee. "Remember that."

He looked at her questioningly, but that was all she said.

An hour later, Jonathan was in the field picking cotton. He heard a shout. It was Roy, bounding toward him from the road.

Jonathan waved listlessly, the sack of cotton hanging from his shoulders.

Reaching him, Roy tipped back his cap, his eager smile fading. "What's wrong?"

"Nothing."

"You look green," Big Roy said bluntly.

Jonathan shrugged. He told him about the snake.

"Well, it's good you got it before it got you."

"Yes. So—" Jonathan mustered a hearty tone. "Mr Nockle gave you a day off?"

"No."

"No?"

"No. I've run away."

"*What?*" Jonathan stared at him in concern. "Why?"

Roy poured out his grievances. He would never get used to working indoors from morning till night, hated the work, hated the city. Mr. Nockle closed the café early in the evening—the riverfront saloons and gambling houses got all the later business anyway—but then there was nothing to do.

"Nothing to do!" Jonathan exclaimed incredulously. "In *New Orleans?*"

"I'm not one for nightlife. I like peace and quiet."

His complaints went on. The café was especially busy right now because a big steamer was in port for a few days. The crew favored Mr. Nockle's gumbo, so they crowded in.

"Mr. Nockle says they want a friendly atmosphere, not just a good meal. He tells me to make them feel welcome, but I don't know how." Roy added bitterly, "I'm wasted there."

"But—where will you go?"

The taller boy shifted, looking uncomfortable. "I thought maybe Mr. Tilden could use an extra hand to pick the cotton crop."

"A field hand? You want him to hire you?"

"I was hoping."

Jonathan knew Pa had no money to pay an extra hand. "Did you tell Mr. Nockle you were leaving?"

"No. I just left."

"How can the man manage, with no notice?"

Roy shrugged indifferently. "Dunno, but I'm gone for good."

Jonathan's thoughts raced. He imagined the Scaly Minnow crowded with friendly faces, and the Nockles, cheerful but beleaguered, trying to keep up with the orders, cooking, clearing tables, serving, settling up bills.

He proposed to Roy, "Look, don't decide anything too fast. You might feel different next week."

"I'm sure I won't."

"Anyway—you're here, and Mr. Nockle needs help in New Orleans. Suppose I turn up at the Scaly Minnow and give him a hand? I'll ask Pa if we can trade jobs for a few days."

"Not mention that I've run away?"

"That's right, keep it simple. I doubt Pa'll have any objections. He'll get the cotton crop in faster with you here, anyway." Jonathan's plans spun on, kindled by this unexpected opportunity. "I won't ask for the wagon. I'll walk, if you tell me the way."

"That's easy, but—suppose Mr. Nockle sends you back?"

"Why would he? He's got to have help," Jonathan pointed out. "And besides—"

"What?"

"I just don't think he will."

·{ **13** }··

Brett Nockle was no fool. When Jonathan appeared at the Scaly Minnow in the middle of the afternoon and tried to skim through an explanation of why Roy had disappeared—"He meant to ask your permission, sir, but he forgot"—the man's eyes narrowed.

He demanded, "Roy's run off, hasn't he, lad?"

"In a way."

"And you want to take his place."

Dusty, tired from the long walk, Jonathan twisted his cap in his hands and agreed, "That's about the size of it, sir."

"Does Mr. Tilden know?"

"He knows I'm here. I have his permission to stay till the end of the week, and Roy's picking cotton on our farm."

Mr. Nockle considered this. He broke into a laugh. "A pretty good arrangement."

Relieved, Jonathan laughed, too. "We thought so, sir."

They were standing in the kitchen. A pot boiled

over. Mr. Nockle darted to the stove to attend to it.

"You didn't bring any extra clothes?"

"A few. And my banjo. I left them outside."

Amused, Mr. Nockle said, "You can bring them in."

Jonathan hesitated. "Should we ask your missus?"

"It'll be all right."

Jonathan fetched his things.

"Put those in Roy's room," Mr. Nockle told him. "It's through that door. There's a sink and water closet in the back."

"I'll wash up, then."

"Do that. The supper crowd'll be coming in. And, Jonathan?"

"Yes, sir?"

"You're a smart lad. You've got a lot of moxie. Just be sure you don't get *too* smart."

A little taken aback, Jonathan replied, "Oh, no, sir."

"You're on trial. You understand?"

"Yes. Yes, I do."

Jonathan reflected that now he was on trial in two places, here and the Tildens'. What would happen to him if he failed these trials, he had no idea.

Much as he yearned to explore New Orleans, Jonathan stuck close to the Scaly Minnow in that week.

Even after the café had closed at night, he offered to rearrange shelves, or fry a batch of doughnuts, or polish pots. He never touched his banjo, not wanting to be thought frivolous or irresponsible.

Each morning he rose at dawn to set the tables and cut vegetables for gumbos and fritters, and he was quick with a smile and fresh coffee when the early customers came in. Only once did he take a few minutes for himself, and that was when Mrs. Nockle sent him to the docks to buy fresh fish.

It was early in the morning. She had told him exactly what to buy and what to pay, and Jonathan made the purchase quickly from a fishing boat just in. Then, with the gutted silver fish weighting his pails, he paused to watch the sun climb over the river mist. Every toot of steamboat whistles puffed forth a little ghost of steam. Veils of golden light brightened and shifted. Gulls, their white feathers glowing, seemed to fly through a dream landscape, and the water looked soft as smoke.

Jonathan breathed deeply, exhilarated by being out here alone in the morning air. The rich river smell was salted with smells of fresh fish and burning coal, and, it seemed to him, of far places. He imagined the whole great ribbon of the Mississippi, flowing to a hundred ports, a thousand adventures. His spirit stretched wide.

He thought of Kyle Foss; even looked around the docks for a red head and a crooked grin. He hardly expected to see him, and did not, but his glance grazed the young bootblack he had noticed on his last trip to New Orleans. Threadbare and pinch-faced, the boy caught Jonathan's eye, smiled tentatively and started toward him.

Jonathan was wearing his new Levi's, a clean red-checked shirt, and his city cap. He had left his big straw hat in Meander Creek. He prided himself that he had the appearance of a reasonably prosperous working person, not a waif or a country bumpkin. The boy, who looked unhealthy and underfed, reminded him unpleasantly of his past.

Deliberately he looked away. He greeted a barge captain with a cordial, "Good morning," as though they were friends and equals, then strode purposefully back to the Scaly Minnow.

Jonathan went home to Meander Creek at the end of the week, fearing that otherwise Ma and Pa would fetch him and never let him go again. And he persuaded Roy to return temporarily to New Orleans. But before long, the boys arranged to change places again. Seeing that the work was done better than before, neither Mr. Nockle nor Pa Tilden objected.

Soon the visits stretched to a week or two, then

longer. During one of his times at home, Jonathan realized Ma was offended by his long absences. Her requests for his help were always soured by comments like, "If it's not too much to ask," or, "Unless you're worn out already."

Discomfited by her resentment, he chose a moment when she was alone in the kitchen and told her warmly, "Ma, I'm aimin' to come back here to the farm real soon! To stay, I mean. I'll be milking the cows again. I'll split wood for you," he added, because this was a job he had always lagged on in the past. "You won't have to tell me twice!"

Her cool blue eyes met his appraisingly. "Maybe it'll be that way. Maybe it won't," she sniffed.

Eugenie was even more outspoken. She cornered Jonathan in the barn and demanded, "When are you coming home?"

"Why, I'm here right now, Eugenie."

"For keeps, I mean."

"I—well, I don't know. Why?" Making a joke of it, he asked, "Have you missed me?"

"It's not that. It's worse than missing somebody. It's—you've given away your family! We're Roy's family now." Her round face reddened with hurt and accusation. "That's about the worst thing a person can do."

Jonathan was dumbfounded. "Don't say that."

"It's true." Her brown eyes glistened with tears. "I don't even like Roy, and now I guess he's my brother."

"No, no, of course not," Jonathan protested, plunged into more guilt and confusion. With hardly a thought, he had been leaving the farm, returning, leaving again, utterly unaware of anybody's pain. What had gone wrong?

"Why don't you like Roy?" he asked, hoping to deflect the argument.

"He's too tall," Eugenie stated defiantly.

"Eugenie, you can't not like a person because he's too tall. It doesn't make sense."

"Don't tell me how to feel!"

"No, no—I'm sorry. I just mean you might give him a chance."

"Why? Is he staying forever?"

Jonathan's temper rose. "I don't know! Let it be!"

His chief concern was that Roy would start feeling unwanted and head off to another farm, or even decide to reclaim his old job at the Scaly Minnow. This didn't happen. By prearrangement with Jonathan, Roy faithfully took an occasional turn of a few days' work at the café, but he preferred Meander Creek. Leaner, browner, clearly content, Roy settled even deeper into farm life.

$\overset{\textstyle .\ .\ .\ .}{\text{A}}_{\text{t}}$ the end of November, Mr. Nockle began giving Jonathan a small weekly wage. The Tildens had never done this. Occasionally they had bought him small gifts—marbles, a mumblety-peg knife, a bristle brush to tame his thick dark hair. But a weekly wage was different. Jonathan was delighted to have money to spend any way he chose.

Going to and from Meander Creek, he sometimes detoured through the French Market and treated himself to a sugary *beignet* and a cup of *café au lait*. He walked along Rue Royale, where a famous singer, Adelina Patti, had once stayed, and past fashionable Antoine's Restaurant on Rue St. Louis. He imagined himself wealthy.

One morning on his way to the café, he saw a banjo in the window of a pawnshop. It had a woven cotton strap to wear over a shoulder, very handy if a person played standing up.

Since coming to New Orleans, he had thought little about his playing. Suddenly he wondered if he had enough money to buy a strap like that.

On impulse, he entered the shop. A clerk came forward. Jonathan explained what he wanted, and the clerk offered him a strap similar to the one in the window.

"What's the price?" Jonathan asked.

"Ten cents."

"Good enough." He brought out his money and made the purchase. "Thank you."

That day Jonathan exerted himself to be more useful than ever in the café. Tirelessly he bandied quips with the customers, zipped through every job he could do in the kitchen, swept the café until even the hungriest mouse would find it bare. He arranged and rearranged the free bread and piccalilli on the tables.

"Looks as if he's going to start swabbing down the walls any minute," one customer commented to Mrs. Nockle with a chuckle.

Another lunchtime regular, a riverboat gambler, joked, "I'll wager a dollar this boy has something on his conscience! Never saw a harder worker!"

"It's just the extra energy I get from drinking Mr. Nockle's coffee," Jonathan parried with a quick grin.

Everybody laughed, including Mr. Nockle himself. The Scaly Minnow was known for the strength of its coffee, which, some said, would raise the dead.

When they had closed the café that night, Jonathan raced through his usual chores. Then he tucked his banjo under his arm, with the new strap over his shoulder. Summoning all his courage, he knocked on the door of the Nockles' huddle of rooms, which were next to his own in the back of the café.

"Come in."

Jonathan opened the door. Mr. Nockle was sitting at his big desk, the café's account book open before him. He looked at Jonathan above the wire-rimmed spectacles he wore for close work. "Well, what favor are you about to ask?" he inquired jovially.

"I just want to go out for a while, sir."

"Oh? Where to?"

"To Rue Bourbon. I've heard they play music there."

"What, you think I'd let you go to one of those honky-tonk saloons?"

"Oh, no, sir. I just want to hear the street performers. I was one myself, once."

"Riff-raff."

"Yes, sir," Jonathan said humbly.

"Drifters without jobs."

"I understand they play some good music, though, Mr. Nockle." His yearning strengthened his pleading voice. "I've hardly seen anything of the city. I want to go very much, sir."

Mr. Nockle gestured to the banjo. "And to play?"

"No, I'm not good enough for that. I'm just hoping to learn," Jonathan replied truthfully.

"Well . . ." Mr. Nockle tapped his pen on his desk,

considering the request. "I'm not sure what Walter Tilden would say."

Jonathan's hopes sagged. "No, sir."

"But—" Mr. Nockle paused. Jonathan held his breath. "Go ahead. Just don't stay out late, hear?"

"No—no, I won't!" In an excited flurry, Jonathan was out the door.

·{ **14** }·

A moon and stars were scattered over New Orleans that night, but Rue Bourbon scarcely needed them. Its gas lamps glowed. Street performers had their own lanterns near them on the raised sidewalk. Light and noise spilled from the open doorways of music halls and saloons in an exuberant jumble.

Small crowds ringed each street performer, clapping, stamping, shouting encouragement. Jonathan paused to watch a clog dancer. Outside a saloon, he heard a honky-tonk piano. A trumpet blasted from the next doorway. Up the street, a raucous voice was swinging through a song.

Then Jonathan heard the sound he was hoping for—the loud twang of a banjo. He ran up the street, his own instrument bumping under his arm.

The banjo player was an old man, sitting on the sidewalk. Jonathan crept closer until he was right beside him. In the lantern's glow, the musician's skin was ashy brown. His eyes had a bluish haze. He was thin and bent and frail-looking, but his fingers flew over the banjo strings magically.

He played several more songs, then pushed himself up creakily and nodded to the crowd. They shouted and whistled and applauded. He went around with his cap, and most people put money in it.

He sat down again and turned his cloudy bluish-brown eyes on Jonathan. In a papery voice, he asked, "You want to play along with me, boy?"

"I can't," Jonathan admitted. "I could never do half what you do."

The old man nodded, accepting that. "You just feel like watchin' and listenin'?"

Jonathan nodded.

"Well, you're welcome."

"Thank you."

Jonathan listened, enthralled, for half an hour or so. Then, remembering Mr. Nockle's admonition not to be late, he slipped away and returned to the Scaly Minnow.

It became a pattern. Each evening when his work was done, Jonathan tucked his banjo under his arm and headed for the bright street. He found out that the old banjo player's name was Billy Barto. A few years back, he had played in St. Louis, at the famous Silver Dollar Saloon. Now he traveled from one riverfront town to another, as the spirit moved him.

Billy knew many of the black musicians who were

creating new music along the Mississippi. He told Jonathan about twenty-year-old Scott Joplin, who played ragtime piano.

"I'm not sure what ragtime means," Jonathan admitted.

"Lookee there." Billy pointed up the street. Two black performers were dancing. Their steps were part shuffle and part stomp, with odd off-beats. The catchy rhythm was accented by hand-clapping and yelps of delight from the onlookers, and from the dancers themselves.

"You get all that goin' together, it's called a rag," Billy explained. "You wanna play a song in ragtime, you do like this." He showed Jonathan how to improvise the extra beats with quick strokes across the banjo's short, unfretted string—the drone string.

Night after night, Jonathan sat by Billy Barto. Gradually he learned different techniques—finger-picking, the nail-brush downstroke, the slide.

One night Billy encouraged him to play a tune for the crowd. The old man took a short break, and Jonathan let loose with "Oh, Susannah!"

"*Ring* that banjo, boy!" cried Billy in a cracked shout. "Ring, *ring* that banjo!"

As he played better, Jonathan began hanging around outside open music hall doors, learning popular songs. He especially liked sentimental ones that told a story. "How dear to my heart are the scenes of my childhood," a performer would sing, and tears would prickle behind Jonathan's eyes.

He had never done much singing, since he had a whistle in his mouth too often. Now he tried it, accompanying himself on the banjo.

Finally he played and sang his own rendition of "The Old Oaken Bucket" for Billy Barto. His voice was loud and true, and he sang with feeling.

The old man responded with his highest praise: "You're ready with that one! Sing it for the folks!"

Whenever Jonathan earned a few extra coins this way, he returned to the café with a bounce in his walk and a jingle in his pocket, feeling like a millionaire. Between wages, tips, and occasional street-performing money, he saved up and bought a new pair of shoes. Now his feet, shod in luxurious leather, seemed almost to dance down the street.

The next week, seeing that one was slightly scuffed, he walked to the docks and looked up the young bootblack. Jonathan summoned him with a snap of the fingers and a wave, as gentlemen did. He got a shine. He tipped the boy a little more than average.

"Thank you." The boy pocketed the money and gave the boots an extra swipe. He asked, "You work at the Scaly Minnow, don't you?"

"I do," Jonathan replied negligently.

"You're lucky."

Jonathan knew there were many homeless, jobless people in New Orleans. He nodded.

"My name's Rowan," the boy told him. "If you hear about a job I could do, let me know."

"Sure thing."

A few days later, some stale doughnuts were left over in the café. Instead of throwing them away as usual, Jonathan took them instead to Rowan. He gobbled them gratefully.

Jonathan thought of old Mr. Cassidy in the grocery store in New York, who had been kind to him so many times. As he stood here in the sun, healthy and well-fed, wearing new boots and giving food to a bootblack, those days seemed very far away.

At Christmas, Jonathan bought presents for Ma and Pa and Eugenie, and spent the holiday with them. Roy was there, too. He slept on a moss-filled tick in Jonathan's room. The Nockles had closed the café for a few days to visit relatives.

There were some changes on the farm. Millard had gone to work for the Southern Pacific. Joseph, the new field hand, wasn't especially friendly, so Jonathan had no more sociable chats outside the little cabin.

Eugenie could read better now. With only occasional help from Ma and Pa, she read "A Visit from

St. Nicholas" to the family on Christmas Eve. Then they all decorated a pine tree with homemade paper chains and ornaments.

It was a nice Christmas. But that was Jonathan's last visit to Meander Creek for a while. He had survived the great blizzard, the trip on the Orphan Train, the rattlesnake. He was glad to see the last of 1888 and to make a fresh start.

His evenings on Rue Bourbon continued to be full and joyous. However, his days at the Scaly Minnow worsened.

At first, knowing he had to get up early, he had been very careful to return to the café before the town clock struck ten. Then sometimes it got to be eleven. Then midnight.

Absorbed in the music, he forgot everything else. Finally he tore through the streets like an addled Cinderella.

Often he overslept the next morning, and was in a scramble of unreadiness when the first customers came to the café. This put Mrs. Nockle into a temper. At her insistence, Mr. Nockle cut his weekly wage each time he was late, once eliminating it altogether. Jonathan didn't really blame them. He had considerable respect for money, and thought he would do the same thing in their place.

Yet he was still late. The old sense of inner dis-

traction took hold of him again, as he swept the café floor, swabbed the tables, cut up vegetables.

One morning, short of sleep and smarting from a tongue-lashing by Mrs. Nockle, he rushed to wait on a customer and knocked a cup of hot coffee into the man's lap.

"Watch what you're doing, you clumsy lad!" the customer roared, jumping up.

"Oh, sir, I'm sorry—so sorry—" Jonathan tried to swipe at the man with his slop cloth, but the angry customer swatted him off. Mr. Nockle rushed forward with extra napkins.

Mrs. Nockle cursed under her breath, then railed at Jonathan, "Late again last night! No use this morning!" She turned on her husband. "How long will you keep him on here? The boy's a shiftless no-good!"

Jonathan's face paled. He threw his cloth onto the floor. In a cold fury, he said, "Don't call me that."

"It's what you are!" Again Mrs. Nockle scolded her husband. "Didn't I tell you it was no use taking in one of these orphans? First the big half-wit, now this shifty, lazy—"

"You're being hard on the boy," Mr. Nockle protested.

"I'm not shifty or lazy!"

"He's young. Careless, maybe—" Mr. Nockle put in apologetically.

"Yes. Well." The customer, calmer now, sat down again and attempted a smile. "It was an accident, after all. Bring me some more coffee, lad, and let's say no more about it."

Jonathan obeyed. But from that day, Mrs. Nockle berated him on any excuse. Once she taunted, "Maybe you'd like to go back to living on the streets, Mr. High and Mighty. Would that suit you?"

Jonathan felt like replying, "Yes, I'm off, and be damned to you." But fear stopped him. He had become used to better living. He never wanted to be a beggar again.

He answered with cool politeness, "No, ma'am. I want to stay here. I'm obliged to you for your kindness. . . . I've gutted the catfish. Shall I roll them in cornmeal now?"

In March, Jonathan returned to Meander Creek for a few days to help with the spring planting. Roy also remained at the farm. The Tildens had asked if possibly both boys could work there for a short while, as the field hand Joseph had quit, and the crops had to go in.

The Nockles agreed so cheerfully that Jonathan was worried. He walked slowly to the farm, carrying his banjo and a bundle of clothes, his boots gray with the dust of the road. The farther he got from New Orleans,

the more worried he became. He thought of the many nights he had been late, the times Mrs. Nockle had been furious with him—not without reason, he had to admit.

He remembered his early days at the Scaly Minnow, when customers had praised him and joked with him, and even the owner's wife had given him frequent nods of approval. All that had changed, he realized, almost without his volition. Music had possessed him. The Scaly Minnow, once so attractive, was drudgery now. He had started having the old Orphan Train nightmares again, riding, riding, never getting where he was going.

His rebellion had grown stronger every day. And the Nockles' impatience with him had grown stronger, too.

It was almost a relief to be at the farm again, out of the café. Though Roy now had the bed in their room, and Jonathan had to make do with the tick on the floor, he slept soundly and wakened before dawn. The old routine—milking cows, working in the fields, filling the woodbox—gave him a weary satisfaction.

One evening after supper, he took his banjo outside, as he used to do. He sat beneath a blooming dogwood tree and practiced a new song: "The empty-hearted rover / leaves every door unlatched / and wanders, solitary, his heartstrings unattached . . ."

Jonathan had thought he was alone, but when he finished the song, a small voice behind him said, "You're really like that, aren't you, Jonathan?"

He turned. Eugenie was sitting beside the pond a few feet away.

"Like what?"

"An empty-hearted rover."

Stung, he put down the banjo. "Of course not."

She shrugged and went into the house.

Upset and annoyed, he tried to resume playing, but now he didn't feel like it. The frogs were making a lot of noise. And sudden footsteps made him start. He swung around. It was Binch.

"Come to the treehouse!" Binch whispered. "I have news!"

"Tell me right here," Jonathan replied in exasperation, but Binch had already slipped away through the orchard.

Jonathan followed him, faintly curious. Had Binch won another spelling bee? Or could his news be really interesting for once?

Under the giant live oak tree, he left his banjo on the ground. He climbed up into the flimsy treehouse, grumbling, "I'll be glad when you outgrow this thing."

"You'll never guess what happened!" Binch whispered, conspiratorial even when no one could possibly overhear.

"No, but you'll tell me, won't you?" Jonathan straightened out his long legs, dangling them over the side.

"A Children's Aid agent was here!"

Startled, Jonathan exclaimed, "What! When?"

"This afternoon. He talked to me and the Ashleys. I guess he'll be over at the Tildens' tomorrow."

"But why? What does he want?"

The visit, Binch explained, was to see how the orphans were getting along with their new families. Nearly a year had passed since they were placed out, on trial. Now, if both sides agreed, the families had a chance to make these adoptions permanent.

"Of course the Ashleys want to keep me," Binch reported smugly. "And I want to stay."

Jonathan had been vaguely aware that this time of decision would come, but he had not known exactly when or how. A bleakness descended on him. He had never told the Children's Aid Society about his adoption by the Dales, or his years in the Foundling Home. He had simply said he was abandoned and had lived on the streets from an early age. This was the life story of so many children in New York that he felt sure they had accepted it.

Even now, confronted with another legal adoption, he did not expect trouble on that score. His concern was that he was not exactly part of the Tildens' household, and not exactly part of the Nockles' either, and didn't know what either couple would say about him.

"Well, you'll find out soon enough," Binch snickered.

That night, for the first time on the farm, Jonathan lay sleepless for hours, filled with dread.

·{ **15** }·

Despite his short night, Jonathan was wide awake, alert with apprehension, long before it was time to milk the cows.

He dressed and went out into the fresh dark. It was the second week in March. He remembered that just a year ago, four boys he knew had died or disappeared in New York, in the awful blizzard. He had been near death himself. Now the smell of spring, of mud and vigorous growth, was all around him, a wonderful smell. He had never appreciated the farm smells before, at least not enough. He had been a fool.

All that day, he expected to be called in from the fields to talk to the Children's Aid Society agent, but the call never came. He didn't know if the agent had spoken to the rest of the family. He asked Roy at bedtime, but Roy knew no more than he did.

Pa had hired a new field hand. The next morning, Jonathan was sent back to the Scaly Minnow, still in suspense.

A day or two later, a stranger was waiting for him in the café one morning when he brought in a load of fresh fish from the docks. He was a pleasant-looking man, wearing a dark business suit. He introduced himself as Mr. Harris, from the Children's Aid Society, and got right to the point: "I've spoken to the Tildens and the Nockles, Jonathan. Now I'd like to talk to you."

"Oh, yes, sir." Jonathan tried not to act rattled. "I'll just put the fish in the kitchen, shall I?"

"Do that."

There were no customers yet. Both Nockles were in the kitchen, preparing food. Mr. Nockle took the pails of fish, saying amiably, "You just relax outside, lad. Sit down. Talk with the gentleman."

Mrs. Nockle gave Jonathan a rare smile. She looked pretty when she smiled. "I'll bring you each a piece of pie."

"Thank you," Jonathan whispered, terrified by all this consideration. He returned to Mr. Harris and they sat at a table.

Again the agent was direct. The Tildens wanted to adopt Eugenie and Roy, who were equally willing. The Nockles did not want to adopt anyone at this time, but were agreeable to letting Jonathan stay on at the Scaly Minnow, still on trial. His case would be reviewed some months from now. How did that strike him?

Jonathan licked dry lips. What it came down to was that he had been rejected by both sides. Yet unexpected relief seeped into him, past his humiliation. He was free. He had a roof over his head, food in his stomach—yet he also had possibilities.

"Do the Nockles treat you well?" Mr. Harris asked.

"Oh, yes, sir. Very well."

All smiles, Mrs. Nockle brought out two pieces of pie, silently put them on the table, and slipped off to the kitchen again.

"A lovely lady," Mr. Harris remarked.

"Wonderful," Jonathan said fervently.

"Well, then. Is it agreed? You stay with the Nockles for the time being, and then we'll see. No obligation on either side. Fair?"

"Fair."

In early April, Jonathan was sweeping the floor of the Scaly Minnow when he heard a steam calliope playing on a boat on the river. It shrilled out "Oh, Dem Golden Slippers." Enjoying the jaunty tune, Jonathan swept in time to it. After it stopped playing, he heard a marching band.

This was not unusual in itself. Such bands were well-loved in this city of music. They played in parades and funeral processions, and on practically any public occasion. Jonathan often went to hear them in the park on weekends, but he had never heard one so near the

Scaly Minnow before. It seemed to be right down the street, its big brass drum booming, tuba oompah-pah-ing, cornets and clarinet blaring.

There was another sound mixed in with the instruments, a metallic clash that he couldn't place but which seemed familiar.

He threw down his broom and ran to the door. The marchers came around the corner from the levee. They were wearing bright red jackets resplendent with gold buttons and braid. Their pants were ordinary, but they wore perky scarlet caps—except the baton twirler, who loomed tall in a shaggy black shako. The fur hat was held on with a strap under his chin and wobbled unsteadily. Still, he spun his baton with nonchalant skill.

Small children, running from doorways, saw him leading the others and were impressed.

"Lookee! Lookee!" they cried.

Other people ran out, calling to one another, nudging each other, their smiles alight.

The marchers came nearer, the music grew louder. Jonathan's gaze was caught by a mop of red curls under a scarlet cap, and by the player's toothy crooked grin. The fellow was banging together a couple of pie tins, producing the tinny clashes.

Jonathan's jaw dropped. It sounded like—it looked like—it *was* Kyle Foss.

Jonathan was too stupefied to yell at him, and the band was so loud Kyle might not have heard anyway. The marchers had passed before Jonathan got his wits together. He asked a little girl, "What band is that?"

"Why, it's the showboat's!" she answered. "Showboat's in!"

People began to run toward the river, shouting to their neighbors, "Showboat's in! *Jambalaya*'s here again!" Housewives, shopkeepers, factory hands, bartenders, children—they straggled to the docks in a happy disorderly parade. Jonathan was right with them.

The small showboat, tied up below Canal Street among some shabby shanty boats, shone like candy with fresh white paint and red trim. Its deck was circled with white wooden "lace." Bright red paint spelled out *Jambalaya* in letters three feet high on its side, and brilliant banners flew above the deck.

A little white dog wearing a pleated red ruff around its neck ran up and down the gangway, yapping. Above on the deck, a young blonde woman called down indolently, "Hush up that racket, Doodah. We're fixin' to rehearse in here."

Jonathan saw a poster tacked on a notice-board. It read:

Jambalaya!
The High-Water Mark of
Drama, Mirth, and Melody!
Talented Players,
Up-to-Date Comedians,
Cultivated Singers!
Elegant costumes, Gorgeous Scenery!
Bring the Whole Family!

Next to that was a smaller notice.

Presenting Tonight,
A Mother's Lament.
Starting Saturday, *East Lynne.*

His head pounding with excitement, Jonathan waited on the dock until the band returned. The musicians marched down Canal Street, hot and sweaty in their uniforms, and finished with a fanfare. As they broke ranks and ambled toward the boat, Kyle caught sight of Jonathan. He dropped the pie tins in a clatter of astonishment.

A moment later the boys were yelling each other's names, slapping each other on the back, spilling over with questions and news. Kyle explained that he had been adopted by Captain Ralph Farrell and his wife Velma, owners of the *Jambalaya.* He helped with cooking and cleaning and, like everybody else in the troupe, performed as needed.

"So you're one of the 'talented players'?" Jonathan asked with a grin.

"Usually I'm an 'up-to-date comedian,'" Kyle replied with mock solemnity. "Meaning I tell jokes when Champagne Charlie is too drunk to go on."

"Champagne Charlie?"

"Charles Bolind, our chief comic. He's an old minstrel man. He sings a song called 'Champagne Charlie' in his act, and it suits him."

"I see."

"How about you? Ever do any street work these days?"

Jonathan told him about the banjo. No sooner had he gotten the words out than Kyle exclaimed, "What! You're a banjo player?"

"I'm learning."

"Then I wager the Farrells would take you on, quick as a wink! We've got a fiddler and a bones man, but no banjo! We need one!"

"You do?"

"Of course. Every showboat needs a banjo player!"

"It does?"

"Why, sure!" With his usual vitality and resourcefulness, Kyle immediately improvised a plan. "You can give me a hand with my chores, too. Especially the food. Our assistant cook just quit." He confessed, "Frankly, we need all the help we can get. We can't compete with the big 'floating palaces,' like the *Cotton Blossom* and the *Sensation*. We just try to get into ports ahead of 'em, pick up some business, and then move on."

He explained that the *Jambalaya* charged less for its shows than more splendid showboats did. "The Farrells can't pay the troupe much, so we're always short-handed. What d'ya say, Jonathan, want to come aboard and meet Velma Farrell? She's the one who really runs the show."

"Sure!"

They ran up the gangway to the showboat's main entrance, a roofed porch that led into a narrow corridor. Here people were lined up to reach the small stateroom that served as a box office.

"Looks as if we'll have a full house tonight," Kyle said.

He and Jonathan pushed through the ticket buyers to the theater.

Jonathan stood still. He had been in theaters only a few times in his life. Stirred, he took in every detail. The auditorium was fitted with a dozen rows of seats on each side of a center aisle. There was an elevated stage. Directly in front of it was a shallow orchestra pit with an upright piano in it.

Onstage, two women confronted each other. One

was the slender blonde girl Jonathan had seen on deck earlier.

The other was taller, older, more commanding. As Kyle and Jonathan watched and listened, she warned dramatically, "My darling daughter, he is a gambling scoundrel! He will bring you to ruin and despair!"

"I shall hear no word against him, Mother," the girl declared, holding her hands over her ears and rolling her eyes to heaven. "He is *my* true love and I will follow where he leads!"

The other woman dropped out of character and instructed, "Nettie, y'all can bear down on *true* or *love*, but not on *my*. Let's do it again."

Jonathan watched, mesmerized, as the situation unfolded. He sympathized with the mother's fears, shared the daughter's anguish, foresaw worse trouble ahead. The scene ended with Nettie vowing, "Beware, Mother! If I am parted from him, I shall perish by my own hand!"

After a moment's pause, both actresses stepped out of their roles and away from each other. Seeing Kyle, Nettie asked him, "Is there any lemonade?"

"No, it's all gone. Velma, this is my friend Jonathan. He was on the Orphan Train, too, and he never got settled, exactly."

Velma Farrell smiled. "Why was that, Jonathan?"

He fumbled, "It's—it's a long story, ma'am. I do have a job, though."

"But not the *right* job," Kyle shot back. "He's just slinging hash. Velma, this is the answer to our prayers. Jonathan is a *banjo player*."

"And a lover of boats," Jonathan put in.

"Oh?" There was new interest in her tone. "Did you bring your banjo?"

"N-no, I just—Kyle and I only—"

She shook out a lacy handkerchief and touched her forehead with it. The morning was getting hot. "You want to try out for a job on the showboat?"

The suddenness of the question threw him off. "I—I guess—"

Kyle nudged him sharply, and Jonathan ended, "Yes. I do."

Velma asked, "Can you play for me later today? About four o'clock?"

Jonathan realized the café was usually empty at four. It was a good time to get away. "I certainly can, ma'am."

She nodded again and left the stage, followed by Nettie.

Jonathan heard Doodah barking somewhere. "Oh, hush up." Nettie's voice trailed languidly behind her.

Still bewildered, Jonathan turned to Kyle and said dazedly, "This has all happened very fast."

"Seize the moment!" Kyle urged him. "You may never get another chance!"

"But what'll I play?"

"A song with lots of sentiment. That's what our audiences like best."

"I'm going to wake up and find out this is a dream."

"Be prepared. It may be real."

"You're right. I'm on my way."

Jonathan flew back to the Scaly Minnow. Like a whirlwind, he swept the floor and set up the tables for lunch. Luckily the Nockles were at the market this morning. When they returned, he had the café in good order and was greeting lunch customers.

The lunchers cleared out around three. Jonathan washed dishes and set up for the dinner crowd. At ten minutes to four, he slipped out the back door with his banjo, trembling and elated.

As he approached the *Jambalaya,* his nervous joy changed to quaking stage fright. The gangplank looked a hundred miles long. He felt as if he could never walk up it; could never play for Velma Farrell.

Then he remembered telling Ma Tilden he wouldn't go in the kitchen garden again. Ma's reply rang in his head: "You went in the garden today. You met a rattler. Now you're sittin' here eatin' honeyed grits."

Strengthened, he gripped the neck of his banjo and boarded the boat.

·{ **16** }·

On the *Jambalaya*, Jonathan found Velma Farrell and Kyle waiting for him in the auditorium.

Velma asked, "Would you go on up on the stage, please? Pretend like we're payin' customers." She laughed, and sat with Kyle in the fourth row.

Jonathan climbed the few steps to the empty stage. It reminded him of the meetinghouse platform in Laitue last year. But then the other orphans had been beside him. Now, completely alone, he had a moment of pure panic. His banjo hung across his chest on its strap, useless as a dead fish.

Kyle gave him an encouraging thumbs-up. Velma, casual and pleasant, adjusted her wide skirt and smoothed her hair.

"I'm going to play and sing 'Grandfather's Clock,' " he announced stiffly.

"You go right ahead."

Jonathan's vocal chords seemed knotted with fear. He coughed and swallowed. Finally he struck the banjo strings.

With the sincerity he had practiced hard to develop,

134

he sang earnestly, "My grandfather's clock was too large for the shelf, so it stood ninety years on the floor . . . it was taller by half than the old man himself, though it weighed not a pennyweight more . . ."

On through four somber verses he went.

Four times he repeated the fateful chorus: "Ninety years without slumbering (tick, tick, tick, tick), his life seconds numbering (tick, tick, tick, tick) . . ."

And at the end: "It stopped *short*"—he gave the banjo a significant plunk—"never to go again"—another plunk—"when the old man died."

He finished. The song had ended, the clock had stopped, the grandfather was dead, and Jonathan felt pretty worn out himself.

There was a moment of silence. Then Velma said warmly, "I declare, that brought tears to my eyes."

Jonathan let out a puff of relief.

"If I ever heard a real crowd pleaser, that was it," Kyle commented.

"A beautiful song," Velma agreed.

"It seems extra sad when a young person like Jonathan sings it," Kyle pointed out. "I mean, a boy and his grandfather."

"I know a very sad song about a dog, too," Jonathan put in.

Velma nodded. "The men in the troupe all double in brass. Can you do that?"

"Brass?"

"The band," Kyle explained. "Like today, we always march through towns to let everybody know the showboat's in. Then we give a free concert before each show."

"Oh. Well, I play the tin whistle. It's not exactly brass, but—"

"Close enough," Velma said. She asked about his present employment.

Jonathan explained his arrangement at the Scaly Minnow: "No obligation on either side."

"So you could join our troupe if we wanted you to?"

"Yes! I absolutely could."

"We can only pay you four dollars a week, but we never stint on food. Kyle'll tell you that."

"First-rate," Kyle affirmed.

"I'm only getting three dollars at the Scaly Minnow," Jonathan said honestly. He did not add the further truth that he would have worked on the showboat for nothing.

"It's a good life, travelin' on the river." She told him the *Jambalaya* had spent the winter months south of New Orleans, touring the bayous. Now, pushed by their steam tug, the *Rely*, they would work their way upstream through the ports north of here, playing every landing from New Orleans to Baton Rouge, to

Vicksburg . . . Memphis . . . Cairo . . . St. Louis . . .

Every name sounded exotic to Jonathan. He glanced at Kyle, who nodded enthusiastically.

Jonathan hardly dared believe the wonderful images that danced through his brain. To follow spring on the river! To see shows! To have a part, no matter how humble, in putting them on! To be valued as a banjo player, a singer! He felt as if he, Jonathan, had hardly even existed before this moment. It was the happiest of his life.

"Count me in!" he cried.

"Now, wait." Velma smiled. "I'll have to speak to the captain. And you'll have to give notice to your employer."

She explained that the *Jambalaya* needed some minor repairs, and would be here in port for eight or nine days. "If you go with us and don't like showboatin', you'll have a ride back to New Orleans early next fall, weather allowin'."

"I'll like it."

"Don't count your chickens. We have fun, but we have hard times, too."

Jonathan met Captain Farrell later that day. The captain was an immensely tall man with a deep, rolling voice, handsome in his smart blue jacket and captain's hat.

"Mrs. Farrell tells me you knew our Kyle in N'York?" he asked cordially.

"Yes, sir, I did."

"And you want to come with us on the *Jambalaya*?"

"I do."

"Nice, on the river. Lots to see."

They wandered about the topic—Jonathan could understand why it was Mrs. Farrell who ran the show—but eventually the captain said, "Well, we'll be glad to have you. Bring your things on board whenever you want."

With a surge of joy and relief, Jonathan realized it was settled.

His talk with the Nockles was less pleasant, but mercifully brief. Mrs. Nockle's response was simply, "I knew you'd leave us in the lurch."

"I'm not doing that," Jonathan protested. "I'll be around for a week yet. And I'll try to find somebody to take my place, if you want. There's a bootblack on the docks—" He told them about Rowan.

Mr. Nockle nodded. "Tell him to stop by," he suggested affably.

Jonathan spoke to Rowan the next morning. Soon this, too, was settled. Rowan was delighted to start work at once.

Jonathan collected his possessions from the back room. He rolled up the tidy that Eugenie had given him. For the first time in months, he looked at her careful laborious stitches. He remembered Ma's honey cake, and the gift of Levi's which he was wearing at this minute, and the banjo strings that had changed his life.

Feeling sad, he wrapped his clothes in a bundle with his Bible and tin whistle. He had bought several books in the past months, and some sheet music. To his surprise, he couldn't carry all he owned in one trip, but went back and forth a couple of times to the small cabin that would be his on the *Jambalaya*.

Finally there was nothing left to do but say goodbye. Both Nockles were in the kitchen of the Scaly Minnow. He went in, cleared his throat, and said with a quaver, "Well, I'll be off, now."

Mrs. Nockle brushed a strand of hair back from her damp forehead. She mustered a smile and joked wanly, "Don't do anything I wouldn't do."

He laughed. It was a hollow sound, and that was how he felt: like a hollow person.

Mr. Nockle wiped a hand on his apron and offered it to Jonathan. "I wish you well, lad. You know that."

Jonathan nodded. As they shook hands, fresh sorrow rose in his chest. Gumbo was simmering on the stove, the catfish were ready to fry, the first dinner customers would be arriving at any moment. Rowan was out there setting the tables.

Once this had seemed to Jonathan the most desirable place in the world.

The Nockles looked at him with fixed smiles, pausing in their work, obviously trying to be nice while keeping one eye on the cooking. They were ready for him to go. But Jonathan didn't want it to end like this.

He calculated quickly. He had his whole week's wage in his pocket, and most of last week's. The showboat charged thirty cents for tickets in the first six rows, where the rickety wooden seats had thin cushions on them. Back rows were twenty cents. The balcony, for black customers only, cost fifteen cents.

There was a small extra charge for the olio, the variety show that came after the play and ended each evening's performance. Even allowing for that, he could afford to stand treat for the best tickets in the house.

"I'd like to invite you to an evening of entertainment," he told the surprised Nockles.

He proposed that they close the Scaly Minnow early next Monday evening—business was poor on Mondays anyway—and be his guests for the *Jambalaya*'s performance of *East Lynne*.

"*East Lynne!* I've never seen it." Mrs. Nockle's beguiling smile appeared.

"Velma Farrell says it's one of the most popular plays. Very tragic."

The Nockles hesitated, obviously tempted. "Well—" they said simultaneously, then both laughed.

"Thank you, lad," Mr. Nockle said. "We'll look forward to it."

Jonathan knew a tinker in New Orleans who occasionally rode out to the farm country to sell his wares. Sometimes he gave Jonathan a lift to Meander Creek in his wagon. Jonathan arranged to meet him and ride out there to tell the Tildens of his new situation, and to say good-bye.

He dreaded it. He was afraid Ma and Pa would disapprove of his setting off for half a year on a showboat, to do nothing more worthwhile than entertain. But inspired by his success with the Nockles, he decided to invite them to *East Lynne*, too, with Eugenie, and even Roy.

As he jounced over the rutted road, the tinker's pots and pans clanking, his plan grew more splendid. He would treat them to supper at the Scaly Minnow, or perhaps on the showboat itself. This would probably take all the money he had, but he didn't care. He would get the best seats for everybody, and pay the extra charge for the olio. For years, they would remember the good time they had had.

Then he began to worry that the Tildens would refuse. He could hardly imagine them clopping into the city for anything so frivolous. The closer he got to the farm, the worse his idea seemed.

Thanking the tinker, he hopped off his wagon at the place where the road divided, near the bridge, and walked the rest of the way. He passed the Ashleys' handsome house, and the orchard. It struck him that it would be many months before he saw this familiar road again. Maybe he never would.

The Tildens were glad to see him. At supper he told them everything, from the meeting with Kyle, which Eugenie and Roy found especially interesting, to his meetings with the Farrells, and his new job. At first Ma and Pa said little. Then Pa questioned him about what he would be doing.

"Mostly just helping around the boat and playing in the band."

To his relief, Ma and Pa took this calmly.

Then he brought up his invitation. Before anyone else could reply, Eugenie shrieked with delight. Jonathan knew the Tildens seldom refused her anything.

142

Excited glances passed between Ma and Pa. They looked almost young again. "I've never been to a show," Ma said, her eyes bright.

In the end, only Roy decided not to go. He said he'd rather stay here on the farm.

·{ 17 }··

On Monday evening, crowds gathered early along the levee. Gus Gessel, the troupe's youthful calliope player, was playing "Dixie."

The calliope was mounted on the roof of the texas, behind the pilot house. It was powered by steam piped from the *Rely*. Gus wore asbestos gloves, to protect his hands from boiling water that dripped on them as he played. He waved frantically at Jonathan, who was on the deck below him.

Jonathan noticed, but paid little attention. His thoughts were blurred with anticipation of the evening, his first as a host.

He scanned faces on the levee, though he didn't expect his guests yet. The Tildens had decided to carry their supper and eat on the way. The Nockles planned to grab a bite before closing the Scaly Minnow. So probably all of them would arrive just before the play began.

Gus, waving more and more imperatively, finally shouted, "*Jonathan!* Get your band uniform on! This is my last number!"

Jolted, Jonathan gaped up at him.

"I'll play an extra chorus, but *move!*" Gus yelled.

Realizing his tardiness at last, Jonathan raced toward his cabin. It was in the texas, directly beneath the calliope.

This was only Jonathan's third night on the showboat, and he still wasn't used to being in such tight quarters. He took a corner too sharply and bumped into Ronald Renfrew, a senior member of the troupe. Renfrew was made up and in costume for his part as the murderer in *East Lynne*.

"Sorry!" they both exclaimed.

Jonathan darted into his cabin and donned the ill-fitting scarlet jacket and red cap that Velma had given him. Then he joined the other members of the band on shore, where the free concert was to take place.

Farley Sander, the troupe's juvenile lead and baton twirler, gave the starting signal. Jonathan blasted his tin whistle. By his side, Kyle clashed the pie tins together. They marched in place, stepping to the rhythm of the big bass drum, as cornets blared and trumpets tooted.

Just in front of Jonathan, Charlie Bolind, the comic who doubled on the tuba, was weaving slightly—a bad sign, Jonathan guessed, remembering what Kyle had told him about Charlie's drinking habits. Last night and the night before, the comic had gone through his routines flawlessly. He had even played a small part in *East Lynne* with no difficulty, but Jonathan wondered how he would do tonight.

As the band began the second selection for the gathering crowds, Charlie swayed and stumbled. Jonathan grabbed his arm, whispering, "Are you all right, sir?"

Charlie turned a foolish smile on him, and sang witlessly, "Champagne Charlie is my name," though he was supposed to be playing a march on the tuba.

Kyle and Jonathan exchanged uneasy glances.

A minute later, Charlie wandered off, staggering up the gangway to the boat.

Moments later, Velma appeared, costumed and made up for her role as Lady Isabel. She ran to Kyle and Jonathan, said briefly, "I need you both," and flew back up the gangway with the boys behind her. Meanwhile the diminished band played on, as ticket holders lined up to board the boat. Jonathan saw Ma and Pa and Eugenie, with the Nockles close behind them.

To give his theater party an extra touch of class, Jonathan had printed his name on the back of five of the evening's programs, and turned them upside down on the front seats he had reserved. He rushed over to the group, babbled, "Right up front! Look for my name!" and hurried off.

In her rich brown wig and formal gown, Velma met

him and Kyle backstage. She was agitated but composed.

"You'll have to go on for Charlie," she told Kyle tersely. "In the olio, try to come up with some better jokes than last time."

"Right," Kyle agreed promptly. "What about the lighting?"

Various members of the troupe managed the lights as needed, depending on whether or not they had to be onstage during a particular production. This week it was Kyle's responsibility. For the past two nights, Jonathan had been assigned to watch him and learn, and he had tried his best to keep it all straight. But now he had a sinking feeling as Velma turned to him.

"Jonathan will do the lights," she said firmly.

"Oh, now, I—" Jonathan began feebly.

Kyle gave him a bruising jab in the ribs with his elbow.

"Sure enough," Jonathan amended, with a pretense of confidence.

Twenty minutes later, the band concert ended, and the hall was full. Many in the audience, including the Tildens and the Nockles, seemed to be dressed in their best. Others had come directly from a long day in the fields or on the docks, their seamed faces expectant, eyes shining. They looked at the red velvet curtain with wonder, as though it were a show in itself.

The middle section of the curtain had a pastoral scene painted on it. This was the part that would go up when the play began. Two side panels, forming the wings, bore advertisements, one with a picture of a kneeling elephant (*Hamlin's Wizard Oil Cures All Pain, Man or Beast*) and one for Liberty Skin Purifier, a sure remedy for freckles and liver spots.

As the actors took their places behind the curtain for the opening scene of *East Lynne*, Jonathan stood in front of the gasboard, backstage. *"Now,"* Velma whispered to him.

Levers on the gasboard controlled the flow of acetylene gas from its storage tank under the stage. The gas was a modern improvement over oil-burning footlights, but was known to be dangerous. A stray spark could ignite any leak in the tank, and cause an explosion. Last year a boat had burned to ashes after such a catastrophe.

Having heard all this from Kyle, Jonathan had qualms as he pulled the levers. A stagehand touched the jets with an alcohol torch attached to a long pole. The foots and borders flared up without mishap, and the audience exclaimed in appreciation.

"Bunch" lights—groups of gas burners set on a stand where their glow was reflected from bright new dishpans—made islands of extra brilliance onstage, which the actors could step into to deliver big speeches.

Once these were ablaze, Gus Gessel, without his asbestos gloves now, took his place at the piano under the stage.

He was wearing a derby hat, a shirt with arm garters and a fancy silk vest, striped pants, and had a cigar clenched between his teeth. He struck up the signature song of *East Lynne*, the poignant "Then You'll Remember Me."

This music, always associated with the play, brought prolonged applause. The curtain rose.

As the grim story unfolded, Jonathan had belated fears that its subject matter might not be suitable for Eugenie. It dealt with suspected adultery, among other questionable matters. He wondered how Ma and Pa would feel about having their child exposed to such ideas.

He peeked through a slit in a side curtain at one point, and saw Eugenie's rapt face. Ma and Pa seemed to be paying equally close attention, but he couldn't tell what they were thinking.

By the time the play reached its tragic conclusion, there was scarcely a dry eye in the house. Even Jonathan, seeing it for the third time in as many nights, felt wrung out. The curtain calls went on and on—especially for Velma, whose Lady Isabel would, it seemed to Jonathan, melt stone.

Finally Captain Farrell went before the closed curtain and held up his hands for silence. He made his usual speech, thanking everyone for coming and urging them to pay the fifteen cents extra and stay for the olio.

"Our variety show will cap your evening with music and mirth," he promised.

Most people did stay, including the Nockles and Tildens, who had been given their extra tickets ahead of time.

During the intermission, Jonathan dimmed the foots and borders. He climbed up to the center of the balcony, behind the apparatus that controlled the limelight.

Gus Gessel struck up "The Blue Tail Fly" on the piano. Following his cue card, Jonathan tried to focus the spot flood on the stage left entrance. To produce it, he had to blow flames from two gas jets against two pieces of lime. As he did this, the lamp crackled and sputtered. Members of the audience around him watched the process with interest.

Sparks of red-hot lime flew; fragments dropped. Gus vamped gamely on the piano.

The limelight went out, then on again. At last, hissing, it steadied into a strong white circle.

Doodah entered in her red ruff, dancing on her hind legs.

The audience gasped, burst out laughing, and

150

broke into delighted applause. The act was called Doo-dah and her Capering Canine Cuties. Doodah was the only live canine in it. The others were puppets worked by Nettie, who stood behind screens that concealed her from the audience.

One by one the dog puppets appeared and danced, led by Doodah. The little dog, though noisy offstage, was a real trouper while she was on. She never barked, never moved outside the circle of limelight, never reacted to noises from the audience. As the music ended, she stood in the center of the spot, twirled, and exited to cheers.

Jonathan managed to keep the spotlight bright through the magic act, the juggler, and Captain Farrell's rendition of "Rocked in the Cradle of the Deep," a song that showed off the lowest notes of his bass voice. Then, as the captain took his bows, the lime began to sputter again.

On the program, comic Charlie Bolind's act was listed next. Replacing him, Kyle made his entrance just as the limelight went out, leaving the stage—and the performer—in almost complete darkness.

The audience tittered uncertainly. Horrified, Jonathan saw that most of the lime had burned away. He inserted two new pieces in the lamp, his hand trembling. At last he got it burning again.

Kyle, suddenly illuminated, twirled his cane and

chuckled, as though this had all been part of his act. Dressed in a comic's baggy pants, wearing greasepaint and a red false nose, he looked several years older than he was. He began briskly, "Yesterday I went to a wedding. They got married for better or worse—he couldn't have done better, and she couldn't have done worse—"

The limelight sputtered and went out again. In a sweat, Jonathan made certain the pieces of lime touched, and directed the gas flames to the point of contact. The spot finally reappeared on stage, and so did Kyle, though now he seemed somewhat rattled.

"I tell you, this bridegroom is so stupid," he went on, as the limelight crackled and hissed. "Other day he said to me, 'If I only had some ham, I'd have a ham sandwich, if I only had some bread.' "

The light went out, then blinked on again. Kyle blinked, too. He continued in a voice of barely concealed desperation, "See, this fellow keeps looking for ideas, but he never finds any. If you say hello to him, he's stuck for an answer—"

The audience, eager to have a good time, laughed, though perhaps not as loudly as before.

"So at this wedding—at this wedding—" Kyle stammered.

Looking at his face, Jonathan had a ghastly realization that his friend had completely forgotten what he planned to say next. Now the limelight burned beautifully. The silence edged toward restiveness.

Kyle, clearly cudgeling his brains, swung his cane, but did not utter a sound.

Words popped into Jonathan's mind—and, before he could stop them, out of his mouth. He shouted, "Sounds as if your friend is just like a match, know what I mean?" He prayed Kyle would remember the answer; it was one of his old riddles.

Kyle's face broke into a wide grin. "Why, you're right about that!" he called back. "A match has a head, but can't think!"

Now the laughter was louder, triggered by surprise at this new entry into the act.

Kyle went on readily, "I love a riddle!" He spread his arms to the audience. "Anybody else feel that way?"

"Yes! Sure!" some of the customers joined in.

"Tell me the answer to this, then," Kyle demanded. "What goes up and never comes down?"

There was some uncertain murmuring, then somebody said, "Smoke?"

"Absolutely! Very good! Smoke!" Kyle was his old confident self, in full command now. He ran through his repertoire, ending with one of the hardest of all:

"Brothers and sisters have I none, but that man's father is my father's son—who *is* that man?"

When no one else answered, Jonathan obliged by bellowing, *"Your son!"*

Kyle bowed, shook his cane in farewell, and exited to applause.

After the show, Jonathan joined his guests.

"We had the best time," Mrs. Nockle sighed and smiled. "You were real good in your part."

"Thank you." Jonathan doubted if Velma Farrell would think so. He hadn't seen her since before the show, and dreaded her reaction.

Mr. Nockle shook his hand. "You be sure to come see us in the fall, now."

"I will."

When they had gone, Jonathan lingered with the Tildens. Eugenie, leaning sleepily against Ma, said, "The dogs were the best."

Jonathan asked Ma, "I hope the play was all right for—?" He glanced meaningfully at Eugenie.

Ma considered. "Lady Isabel was a married woman. She left her husband and ran off with another man, who turned out to be a murderer. She lost everything. Her child died. *She* died." She concluded, *"East Lynne* is a true moral lesson." Looking down, she added, "Remember that, Eugenie."

Jonathan walked them to their wagon. Pa had hitched the old farm horse on Canal Street.

"It was a fine evening," Pa said warmly. "A fine evening."

With a lump in his throat, Jonathan watched them ride away.

·{ **18** }··

Next morning, breakfast in the low-raftered dining hall of the showboat was late and leisurely. As usual, the Farrells ate at the center table, along with Ronald Renfrew, Nettie, and Farley Sander. Jonathan and Kyle were seated with stagehands and lesser members of the company, while the crew of the steam tug *Rely* had tables of their own, near the kitchen.

Usually Jonathan liked the dining hall. The chatter of crew and actors, the bustle of food being served and china clattering, stirred dim recollections in his mind of the Foundling Home, and made him comfortable. Now, though, he was distinctly ill at ease.

On the way into the room, Velma had stopped him and said, "I need to talk to you, Jonathan. You too, Kyle. Y'all meet me on deck right after breakfast, hear?"

"We'll be there," Kyle replied, sounding somewhat constrained. Jonathan had merely nodded, mute and miserable. Both boys felt they had made a mess of things last night, Jonathan with the lighting, Kyle by forgetting his lines. They sat at their table gloomily, ignoring the chit-chat around them.

Jonathan stole looks at the center table. Nettie's fair hair was still up in rags. Indolent in a rosy wrapper, she held Doodah on her lap and fed the dog bits of bacon, as Farley Sander watched her with a fond smile. Captain Farrell looked immaculate in his blue jacket and white trousers, a head taller than anyone else at the table.

Opposite him, his wife was straight-backed and neatly groomed, wearing a crisp, sprigged morning gown. Her eyes met Jonathan's, but she was as unrevealing as a tree. With the other performers, she lingered a long time over coffee.

Kyle and Jonathan left their table and stood together on deck, waiting.

"Do you think she'll throw me off the boat?" Jonathan asked in a small voice.

"I don't know," Kyle admitted.

"Has she ever done that? Just gotten rid of somebody?"

Kyle nodded bleakly.

They waited. At last Velma joined them. She was not smiling. She looked first at Jonathan, then at Kyle, creating one of the long, dramatic pauses that she used to such good effect onstage.

In a tone of ominous calm, she addressed Jonathan first. "What kind of a performance would it be, I wonder, if we all spoke out durin' each other's acts?"

She waited for an answer.

"Awful," Jonathan croaked.

She turned to Kyle. "And how would it be if we all forgot our lines, every time any little thing went wrong?"

"I just—I—" Kyle stammered.

She fixed him with her commanding gaze. "Well? Wouldn't be much of a show, would it?"

"No," he mumbled, downcast. "It would be terrible."

"I don't blame you for the lightin'," she told Jonathan. "I suppose you did the best you could, and the limelight's tricky."

"Yes, ma'am!"

"But I *do* blame you for lettin' your feelin's get the better of you. I nearly fainted dead away when you started shoutin' out from the balcony, *while an act was in progress.*"

Kyle put in, "Velma, my brain went woolly as a cotton boll. I was *dying* out there."

"Then he should have let you die."

"Yes, ma'am," both boys whispered.

"However—" They both perked up at the change

in her tone. "However, the audience liked it. You know that, and—" She sighed. "I know it, too." She raised a warning finger. "But if you ever do it again, Jonathan Dale, the captain will tar and feather you and throw you overboard for bait. And around here, the fish bite."

Jonathan's apprehension lifted suddenly, leaving him buoyant as a bubble on an updraft. But he didn't dare smile. He nodded gravely.

She went on. "Still, we can't always depend on Charlie. So I want you two to work up some routines. I have a couple of books of skits. Go through them and see what you can find. These are to be performed *onstage*, hear? Not from out yonder all over the theater!"

"Right."

"We'll be leavin' New Orleans Friday mornin', headin' upriver. Remember, Jonathan, we won't be back here till September. Sure you want to go?"

"Yes!"

"All right. The captain plans to put in first at Petit's Landin'. In the meantime, you two can help paint scenery for the play we're doin' there. It has a big burnin' ship scene, Jonathan. We'll need you to burn the ship."

"What?" he asked, startled.

"A scenic effect."

"Oh."

"It's not hard. You stand in the wings and push a cutout of a ship's prow onstage. Then you hold a shovelful of burnin' coals just out of sight. Creates a glow."

For Jonathan, the rest of the week passed in a kaleidoscope of rare and marvelous hours. Though he and Kyle had many menial chores to do, most of their jobs were connected with performances.

They painted scenery under Ronald Renfrew's direction. It was like magic, to paint a scene where imaginary characters would come to life. Adding colors to a bush, a riverbank, a distant house, Jonathan thought of the audiences that would look at it, lost in stories. It seemed to him that a story, once you believed in it, was the most fascinating thing in the world.

In spare minutes, he practiced lyrics he believed would please showboat audiences, asking himself, "How would it feel if your grandfather died? How would it feel to be in love?"

Listening, Velma told him she wanted him to sing three of those songs in the next olio program. "You'll be on the handbill in Petit's Landin'," she told him.

"My name will be in print?"

"It will," she promised.

When she returned from the New Orleans printer, she showed him the handbill, pointing to the place just after Doodah and her Capering Canine Cuties. Jonathan stared at it with a resounding joy that was close to tears. He read the words aloud: "Jonathan Dale. Banjo player."

On Thursday, he and Kyle pored over comedy skits, trying to decide on one, and on which of them should do which part. Kyle could toss out a straight line with some authority, but was hopeless when he had to actually act. Jonathan, though, displayed an exuberant talent for comedy that he had not known he had. He felt as though he had come upon a secret cache of gold.

"How about if I'm the straight man and you're the comic?" Kyle suggested.

"Fine with me."

They tried out a number on Velma, who laughed with gratifying gusto. She warned Charlie Bolind, "Youth is nippin' at your heels, Charlie. Watch your step."

He grinned sheepishly. "The demon rum shall never pass my lips again, Velma."

Kyle whispered to Jonathan, "He always says that."

The *Jambalaya* was late getting off on Friday, waiting for food supplies that hadn't been delivered. Jonathan stood alone by the railing on deck, looking at the morning's activity on the docks. He saw Rowan, a pail in either hand, approach one of the fishing boats and buy fresh catfish. It was a curious feeling, like seeing a little scene from his own life.

He had an impulse to say good-bye, or just to detain the boy for a moment, and called, "Rowan!"

But just then the *Jambalaya's* whistle tooted. Rowan didn't hear him. Picking up the heavy pails, he walked slowly away, toward the Scaly Minnow.

Petit's Landing was a small town, only a few hours upriver from New Orleans. As soon as the *Jambalaya* was tied up at the wharf, Velma gave Jonathan the poster advertising the evening's entertainment. It bore a picture of a large packet boat engulfed in flames, and the words, SEE THE BURNING OF THE STEAMER *MULLOY!*

He tacked up the poster on a notice board near the docks. Two young women watched him. One remarked, "My, the things they can do! Imagine burnin' a steamer onstage!"

"I wonder if Mother would bring us? I'd love to see it!"

"Let's go home and ask!" They hurried off, leaving Jonathan elated, but rather nervous, as the sensational effect depended on him and his shovelful of coal.

Velma had explained that Leroy, the troupe's cook and chief stagehand, would start the coals in the kitchen stove well ahead of time. Meanwhile Jonathan was to wait in the wings. Just before the crucial scene, Leroy would deliver the coals to him, all aglow in a big bucket.

Velma told him, "When I say, 'What is that strange orange glare on the horizon?' you get ready. Then Nettie says, 'It looks like a fire on the river!' and the curtain will close *briefly*. That's your cue. Don't miss it."

He didn't. With the curtain closed, Leroy swiftly changed the backdrop and set a cardboard rock and some bushes in the foreground to simulate a riverbank. Jonathan pushed the cutout of the ship's prow onstage. Ronald Renfrew, as the dastardly villain taking revenge on the woman who has spurned him, took his place behind the rock, wearing an evil leer. Jonathan scooped the coals from the bucket onto the shovel, and stood tense and ready.

The curtain opened again. As Gus vamped ominous chords on the piano, Jonathan held the shovel just offstage. The menacing red-orange glow behind the prow gave the illusion of a ship on fire.

The audience gasped with awe at the spectacle. The distraught mother, played by Velma, made her entrance, clasped her hands in horror, and cried, "No! No! My child is on the *Mulloy!*"

Jonathan held the shovel steady as the actors ran into the wings. They scattered soot over their clothes from a bowl provided by Leroy—to hint at action aboard the burning ship—and ran back onstage. The audience hissed whenever Ronald appeared.

Finally the infant had been rescued, the mother united with her true love, and the villain trapped to perish in the fire—an ending which was greeted with tumultuous cheers.

While the captain made his usual speech in front of the curtain, Jonathan left the coals safely stowed in the bucket, and changed for his number. His nerves were taut. This was his first chance to play and sing for a real paying audience.

He had asked Velma's approval on the songs.

"Just so you don't sing 'Home, Sweet Home,' " she had told him.

"Why?"

"It's bad luck. A boat is bound to end on the bottom of the river by the next sunset, if anybody sings 'Home, Sweet Home' on board."

"Oh. Anything else I should know about luck?"

Gus Gessel, sitting nearby at the piano, put in, "A derby hat is *good* luck. I'll give you one."

So in a dark suit pinned to fit him, and an oversized derby hat, Jonathan appeared before the *Jambalaya* audience.

He twanged the banjo and sang his opening lines. His voice shook at first, but the pent-up emotion of stage fright only added fervor to the song.

" 'Tick, tick, tick, tick—' "

He was a hit. He took two bows, and would have taken a third, but Velma called quietly from the wings, "That's enough, Jonathan."

Jubilant, he stayed awake for hours that night, rocked on the river. In the velvet silence, he kept hearing applause.

·{ **19** }··

While repairing one of her puppets in the morning, Nettie got a sliver of wood stuck in her finger. Velma dug it out, but the finger was sore. Feeling expansive after his success of the night before, Jonathan went ashore to buy Nettie a little cheer-up gift.

Most of the shops were closed—it was Sunday—but he found a street vendor selling candied violets. They were pretty, and Nettie liked sweets. As he stopped to buy a paper twist of them, a buggy passed. He glanced up, and met the eyes of the young girl riding by. Each of them turned their heads, following the other. Then the buggy turned a corner. She was gone.

Jonathan had the distinct impression that he knew her. Her slender face and brown hair, something in the set of her mouth and chin, were instantly familiar. Yet he couldn't recall who she was.

All summer, they trouped up and down the river. In September, when the showboat docked again in New Orleans, Jonathan dropped in at the Scaly Minnow.

"So how do you like the vagabond life, lad?" Mr. Nockle asked him jovially, his wire-rimmed spectacles perched on his nose.

"Must be nice not to do anything but get dressed up and play-act," Mrs. Nockle put in with a touch of malice.

Jonathan thought of the days on the *Jambalaya* when he and Kyle had to swab the deck, clean the cabins, move heavy pieces of scenery, do kitchen chores with Leroy, and worst of all, clean and polish the brass spittoons. But he wasn't going to admit any of that to Mrs. Nockle.

"It's grand," he replied staunchly.

"Soon you'll be too famous to stop by here," she sniffed archly.

"Oh, I'll still stop by when I can," Jonathan said, as though his fame were a foregone conclusion.

Next day he got a ride to Meander Creek with his tinker friend. His visit with the Tildens was short. He had to get back to the boat that afternoon, and wasn't able to wait and see Eugenie, who was at school, or Roy, tilling in a distant field.

In a way, he was glad. It was rare and pleasant to have Pa and Ma to himself. They were sincerely curious about his experiences, and he was more honest with them than he had been with the Nockles.

"Trouping's not easy, but it's interesting," he told them.

"I should say! Goin' from place to place!" Ma exclaimed.

"Travelin's a real education," Pa agreed in his gentle drawl. "I've heard that."

"The towns seem a lot the same after a while, but I love the river," Jonathan said. "It's always different."

"The weather's different?" Ma asked, trying to understand. "The water level changes?"

"That's part of it."

"I reckon you pass through fields and woods and mercy knows what all," Ma said.

"We do. We see the world."

From New Orleans, the *Jambalaya* journeyed south in the fall, through the steaming, swampy bayous. It stopped in remote places where sugarcane and rice grew, and snakes and alligators seemed more at home than people. Small floating chapels plied the back waterways, taking religious services to those who had no church. Little gambling boats worked the landings.

Medicine men sold their wares from ramshackle shanties.

Gus Gessel's music on the calliope always announced the *Jambalaya*'s arrival. Just after dark, Jonathan and Kyle would stick tall kerosene torches along the riverbank. When they lighted them, brilliant flares leaped up. Orange and yellow reflections danced on the river.

From the dark woods and narrow dirt roads, men and women slipped through the shadows, into the glow of the flares. They thronged to the landing, shy and excited, bringing their children and their ticket money. Poor though they were, they came to the showboat.

It gave them drama, romance, glamour. They marveled at the costumes and scenery, wept at the tragedies, burst into guffaws at the comedy. Looking at their faces, Jonathan felt sometimes that no job on earth was better than being an entertainer.

After that first year, he looked forward to winters in the bayous. But going upriver in the spring was splendid, too, when dogwoods shone white against the dark trees. He and Kyle, and Gus Gessel, often spent spare minutes on deck. They watched the river traffic go by, and through Gus, Jonathan acquired a whole new set of dreams.

Though only five years older than he was, Gus was a skilled piano player, and a seasoned trouper. He was saving his money to go to New York City and try his luck in the variety shows.

"New York!" The name lit an old fire in Jonathan. His thoughts swarmed with city memories. "Honestly? Are you really going there?"

"Sure am, soon as I can get enough cash together," Gus assured him. "I'll need train money, then something to keep me going for a while." He added importantly, "Breaking into Tony Pastor's show may be a tough challenge."

Tony Pastor! It was a fabled name in New York. Kyle and Jonathan both knew about Pastor's Fourteenth Street Theater. Opened in 1881, it was advertised as the first specialty and vaudeville theater in America.

Now, in 1890, Pastor's success was lengendary. Largely because of him, variety had become the most popular form of entertainment in the country.

"I used to read about his shows," Jonathan said.

"Who didn't? He's a big man," Kyle agreed.

Pastor had been a child performer, appearing in the circus and in minstrel shows from the age of six. Like Jonathan and Kyle and Gus, he must have learned to captivate audiences when he was very young. It gave them all something in common. Yet it had never occurred to Jonathan that he, too, might be able to be *really* rich, *really* famous, like Tony Pastor.

"When do you figure on going?" he asked Gus.

"In a year or two," Gus answered promptly. "Why don't you fellows come along? You don't want to spend your lives racketing around on this heap, do you?"

Kyle's green eyes sparked with anger. "This heap, as you call it, is a snug little touring company. And we paint her every year."

Gus spread his hands eloquently and shrugged.

Kyle cooled down. "Anyway, the *Jambalaya* is about my speed. I don't have any talent, except maybe for managing things."

"How about you?" Gus asked Jonathan.

"I don't know." Two years was a long way off.

Along the Mississippi, Gus pointed out special sights to Jonathan: a beautiful plantation, looted and burned by Yankee soldiers, its white columns still standing. A prison chain gang in the striped clothes of convicts, ankles manacled together, repairing a levee.

The repairs were a continuous process. Burrowing animals kept damaging the dikes. Crayfish, too, tunneled into them on the river side.

There had been several major floods on the Mississippi in the past decade. Gus had been through one of them.

"When the water went down, you could see all kinds of animals on top of the levee," he told Jonathan. "They had scrambled up there to keep from drowning. Possums, coons, rabbits, snakes—even the alligators got tired of swimming, and climbed to high ground wherever they could."

"Must have been a fantastic sight."

"Like a nightmare. You'd pass a tree, and see a deer up in the branches. Or on top of a house. They hooked on with their legs, however they could. And you'd see the drowned ones floating by, too."

During Jonathan's third year on the showboat, heavy rains swelled the Mississippi again.

When the turbulent weather began, Captain Farrell put in at Petit's Landing. It was not a scheduled stop on this trip—they had hoped to be in New Orleans by now—but the captain and pilot agreed it was too dangerous to go on. The tug pushed the *Jambalaya* into port, and the crew secured it at its mooring.

The storm worsened. Rain and wind lashed the river. Lightning and thunder ripped the sky. Waves tumbled the small showboat like a cork in a maelstrom.

Jonathan lay on his bunk and clutched its sides, to keep from being knocked around the cabin. He was badly frightened. There had been plenty of rough days on the water before, but none as bad as this.

He knew Petit's Landing was more sheltered than the wild open river. There were natural bluffs that had protected it in other floods. Still, he remembered the story about the deer in the tree, and wondered if they would all end like that, with the *Jambalaya* in fragments on the tossing waves.

The storm raged all night, and most of the next day.

Gradually the heavy rain subsided. The troupe began to move around the boat.

Jonathan joined Kyle and Gus on the stage, a communal gathering place, in the late afternoon. Nettie, small and pale, sat huddled on a box of costumes with Doodah in her arms. Leroy, trying to make it seem like an ordinary day, whistled as he went into the kitchen to make coffee.

After a while, Velma looked outside. She said, "Rain's stopping."

They all followed her on deck. A curdled light broke through iron-dark clouds, casting a strange brilliance over the town. Muddy roiling water had spilled from the river to some of the nearby streets. But they were passable, and the houses looked safe.

The troupe members gave each other wan smiles.

Velma said, "Well, since we're here, we might as well do a show."

·{ **20** }·

After supper, Gus Gessel, ready for the evening in his silk vest and arm garters and derby hat, played "Oh, Dem Golden Slippers" to announce the show-boat's official arrival.

Jonathan tacked up a poster on the notice board. The troupe would perform *Ten Nights in a Barroom*, the well-known temperance play.

Charlie Bolind, undone by the storm, had imbibed too much whiskey, and would not be able to appear in the olio. Instead Velma told Kyle and Jonathan to fill in with *The Haunted Barn*.

The troupe extended the free band concert this evening, and started a little later than usual, to give the audience time to get there in the wake of the storm. Just before they began *Ten Nights in a Barroom*, Jonathan, backstage, peered at the audience through a slit in a side panel. Most of the seats in the theater were filled.

The curtain opened. Nettie played a young girl whose drunken father would not leave the squalid bar, even though his little son was mortally ill. Three

times—at one, two, and three o'clock in the morning—
the girl was sent to the bar by her mother, to beg him
to return.

Each time she sang the same pathetic refrain: "Father, dear father, come home with me now—" as Gus
struck emotional tremolos on the piano.

Wispy and delicate, Nettie never failed to move the
audience to tears with the third verse, the climax of
the tragedy:

> "Father, dear father, come home with me now!
> The clock in the steeple strikes three;
> The house is so lonely—the hours are so long
> For poor weeping mother and me . . ."

Nettie's next words confirmed the audience's worst
fears:

> "Yes, we are alone—poor Benny is dead,
> And gone with the angels of light;
> And these were the very last words that he said—
> 'I want to kiss Papa good-night.' "

Through the slit in the curtain, Jonathan peeked
at the audience. Ladies had placed their palm-leaf
fans in their laps, and were clutching damp handker-
chiefs instead. Men wiped moisture from their noses
and the corners of their eyes. There were audible
sobs.

Glancing along the rows, Jonathan's gaze stopped. A young girl in the third row looked hauntingly familiar. Her large, dark eyes and slender face seemed to strike a deep resonance from his past.

She was the girl in the buggy.

But he had known her before that. When?

The play ended. Jonathan got into the baggy pants, red false nose, greasepaint, and fright wig of the comic in *The Haunted Barn*. With Kyle as the straight man, he played the foolish fellow who believes a crazy story about a ghost in a barn.

The straight man taunted him, "You're not afraid of ghosts, are you?"

"Oh, no," Jonathan replied, with a quaver in his voice. "Some of my best friends are ghosts—"

The skit continued to the final moment when the straight man exited and came back on the other side of the stage, draped in a white sheet. In this role, Kyle tiptoed silently across the stage and stood next to Jonathan, who was still prattling. Spying him, Jonathan let out a howl and pulled the string of his fright wig, causing it to stand straight up on his head. The skit ended to much laughter and applause.

Jonathan had a quick change after this, to be ready for his banjo solo. He had no chance to think of the elusively familiar girl in the audience until he was back onstage. Then, near the end of his number, his eyes met hers, and he knew. She was Marguerite, Eugenie's sister.

He wished he could jump off the stage and speak to her, right there and then. But two acts followed his. Only after those, when the audience was rising to leave the theater, he jumped down the stage steps and called, "Marguerite!"

She turned, smiling slightly, a tall and self-possessed young lady of fifteen or so. A man and woman with her turned toward him, too.

"Madam. Sir." Jonathan greeted the older people first, holding on to his manners. Then he said, "Marguerite, I'm Jonathan Dale."

"Yes. I saw that on the program," she said. "I know you, don't I?"

He nodded. "We met on the Orphan Train."

Her large brown eyes darkened. Her face paled. The sprinkling of freckles showed on her nose, but otherwise her face was colorless and still, as it had been when he and Eugenie were taken out of the meeting-house in Laitue.

"You were adopted with my sister," she said faintly. "Is she here?"

"No. I'll tell you all about it, but—" Other patrons were pushing past them to get off the boat. Jonathan asked, "May I call on you at home tomorrow? We'll be staying over another day, at least."

Marguerite looked entreatingly at the older couple. The man nodded slowly. He told Jonathan, "We're at Number Five Decatur. Just up the street. Our name is Merritt."

"Come for tea." The woman smiled. "Four o'clock."

Just one lump, please," Jonathan replied, when Mrs. Merritt asked how much sugar he wanted. He smiled politely, sipping without slurping. The behavior of high-born characters, which he had studied in many plays, was second nature to him now. He seemed calm and poised, but his feelings were a spinning jumble.

Meeting Marguerite after four years had brought back so many other memories. As he gave her the Tildens' address, he could almost see the farm again. He thought of how Eugenie had fed the chickens at sunrise, scattering the cracked corn in cheerful little throws. He remembered his old room—Roy's room, now—with the flypaper by the window. And Pa in the fields. And Ma.

The past few times the *Jambalaya* had stopped at New Orleans, he had not been able to locate his tinker friend. He had not had the leisure or the inclination to walk way out to Meander Creek, and renting a buggy was expensive. Still, he wished he had done it.

Mr. Merritt explained that he had tried to locate Marguerite's little sister, but had failed. Perhaps because so many thousands of children had been placed out, and sometimes moved from one adoptive home to another, they were difficult to trace. Marguerite herself had first been adopted by Mr. Merritt's sister, who had become too ill to keep her.

Jonathan thought of the orange halves and old newspapers that floated on the surface of the river, drifting where the current took them.

"Eugenie's happy at the farm," he told Marguerite, hoping it was still true. "She goes to school. And church. And she has—she has a treehouse."

"So the Tildens love her?" Marguerite asked.

"They do. You can be sure of that."

"We love our girl, too." Mrs. Merritt patted Marguerite's hand. "We'll write Eugenie and the Tildens immediately, and plan a visit, if they're willing."

"I believe they will be," Jonathan said.

In the next months, Eugenie often came into his mind. He imagined her joy and excitement when the letter from the Merritts was received. Ruefully, he realized he had missed several of her birthdays. At last he was giving her a present.

Gus Gessel gave Velma notice that he was leaving for New York in about six months. Leroy, who already had some skill on the piano, agreed to be his replacement. He donned the asbestos gloves, and Gus began teaching him to play the calliope.

There were other changes. Farley Sander and Nettie got married, and soon were expecting a baby. This meant she would not be able to play ingenue leads much longer. A new ingenue named Hyacinth (billed as "The River Flower") was hired in Bayou Teche. Hyacinth had been performing "saucy soubrette" numbers in a café. Velma felt these verged on the vulgar, and told her sternly, "You'll have to keep it clean."

"Yes, ma'am," Hyacinth agreed, her black eyes flashing wickedly.

Kyle was bewitched by Hyacinth. He spent every spare moment teaching her some acceptable songs, analyzing her costumes, even doing errands for her on shore.

"We'll never get him to New York," Gus told Jonathan glumly.

Gus always took it for granted that Jonathan would eventually save enough money to join him in the city. Actually Jonathan hadn't put much aside, though he kept intending to. His wages had been raised year by year, but he liked fine clothes, and never could resist buying flowers or small gifts for friends. Once, before he realized how much Kyle liked her, he took Hyacinth to lunch at Antoine's in New Orleans.

"I'm penniless again," he told Gus ruefully after this extravagance.

Yet he felt things were going well for him. In its small way, the *Jambalaya* was thriving. The showboat had gained a reputation for good entertainment at low prices, and seldom had empty seats. Jonathan and Kyle no longer had to do menial work on the boat. Two new boys had been hired to take over these chores.

In March, Velma dismissed Charlie Bolind after one spree too many, and hired a new comic. Freed from fill-in comedy skits, Jonathan attained the status of featured performer. He had already earned popularity with his singing and banjo playing. Now he often acted in the plays as well.

Gus's plans became definite. He was leaving in April, when the showboat reached Petit's Landing. The train station at Laitue was only a few miles from there.

Jonathan hadn't realized the towns were so close. "Laitue! That's where I got off the Orphan Train."

Gus grinned. "Well, keep saving. Maybe next time through, you'll be jumping on board yourself."

They reached Petit's Landing on a Saturday. Gus hired a buggy and rode to the railway station to buy his ticket. He wasn't leaving until the following Thursday, when the *Jambalaya* would also depart, but he wanted to reserve a place on the train.

He returned to the showboat beaming with excitement. "All set!" He brandished the ticket, and rushed off to change for the evening's performance.

Petit's Landing was a special stop for Jonathan, too. He had decided to call at Decatur Street tomorrow, and find out if Marguerite had seen Eugenie.

Sunday was a mild and lovely day, not too hot. The troupe scattered, to fish, or visit friends, or simply to stretch their legs and enjoy the weather. Only Gus remained on board the *Jambalaya*. Jonathan heard him at the piano, practicing "Sugartown Stomp." It was faster and harder than most of the music he played, and he wanted to use it for New York auditions.

Jonathan dressed carefully for his visit to the Merritts. He wore a gray fitted suit and narrow polished shoes, and bought a flower from a street vendor for his buttonhole. He exuded a fashionable air that had become part of him. At seventeen he was tall and slim, his thick black hair brushed to a gloss. Local papers in the river towns frequently referred to him as "the handsome Jonathan Dale."

Feeling a little nervous, he hummed under his breath as he strolled along Decatur Street. At Number 5, he rapped the brass knocker, and heard footsteps behind the door. It opened. He half expected that Marguerite would be standing there, but the girl was someone else.

He met her clear gaze. Much had changed about her, but that direct look was the same. It was Eugenie.

·{ **21** }··

After a few perfunctory polite minutes with Mr. and Mrs. Merritt and Marguerite, Jonathan and Eugenie both yearned to talk over private memories. They went out for a walk.

Now, alone together, they ambled through town. She told him she and her sister had visited back and forth several times since Jonathan had helped reunite them.

"Tomorrow I'm going back to Meander Creek, so it's lucky you came today."

He agreed, "Yes, very lucky."

"Last night we heard the calliope. I wanted so much to see you, but the Merritts had other plans. And today there was church, and Sunday dinner, and all that. I was going to sneak out later and get onto your boat somehow. Just to say hello and good-bye, for now."

Jonathan smiled. The idea of sneaking out made him think of Binch and the treehouse. "Is Binch still with the Ashleys?"

"Oh, yes. He's keeping company with Mrs. Ashley's niece."

"He is? I can hardly believe it!"

"We're all older, you realize." She gave him a jokingly reproachful smile.

"Yes. Tell me about Ma," he urged her. "And Pa, and the farm."

"Ma's well. She's bothered by arthritis in her hands when she sews, but she made an altar cloth for the church. . . . Pa leaves a lot of farm work to Roy these days. . . . The strawberries are very good this year. . . ."

Wrapped in happiness, Jonathan listened to her lively voice. Content though he was, he swung, unbalanced, between two other sets of feelings. He felt at home with Eugenie, deeply comfortable. They knew each other so well, had shared so much. . . . Yet he didn't really know this older Eugenie. The mystery of her tantalized him and made him bashful.

He glanced at her sideways, taking her in. She wore the sturdy cotton dress of a farm girl. Her long brown hair was loose on her shoulders, held back from her face by a blue ribbon headband. She had grown several inches since he had seen her last. Her round face was subtly changed, though he couldn't tell exactly how. Her strong body curved with the beginnings of womanhood.

He asked abruptly, "How old are you, Eugenie?"

"Thirteen."

"You're older than I was when we first went to the farm. That seems strange, doesn't it?"

"I guess we've had strange lives."

"You'll be a grown young lady soon."

"Yes."

At the edge of town, they turned into a country lane and crossed a sunny field. On the other side, they rested on a fallen log in the shade. Eugenie chewed on a long piece of sweetgrass. Jonathan watched her.

A tension stretched between them, pulling them together, holding them apart.

He said slowly, "I often think of the farm. I wish I had treated you better. I've often wished that."

"You treated me all right."

He smiled, a little sadly. "You're saying I was the perfect brother?"

"No. You weren't perfect. Neither was I. I'm just saying we didn't know how to be part of a family."

"No."

"It caused us a lot of trouble."

He felt as though a serious admission were being wrenched from him. "I still don't know how to. Sometimes it's as if I never got off that train." He hadn't meant to be so serious, and tried to laugh it off. But her answering nod was serious, too.

186

They sat quietly. Bees buzzed in the clover. The sun moved from behind a tree and got in Eugenie's eyes. She said, "We'd better go. The Merritts will expect me at teatime."

He rose, forced a smile, and offered her his hand. She took it and stood. They walked on, hands linked. "Tell me about school," he suggested in a tone that seemed falsely bright, even to him. "Tell me about your friends."

It was a long walk back. Outside Number 5 Decatur Street, he had a terrible reluctance to part from her. She pulled her hand free and stood away from him.

What was she thinking, this mysterious girl-woman with the downcast eyes?

He cleared his throat and said, "The *Jambalaya* will be in New Orleans in the fall. Then I'm going to hire a buggy and ride out to the farm to see you."

She looked up at him quickly, her brown eyes warm. "Maybe we could both go for a ride in it."

"Yes! Yes. I'll take you to New Orleans, if you like."

"I'd love that. I haven't been there very often."

He heard footsteps from somewhere in the house and said quickly, "We'll do whatever you like."

"Do you promise to come?"

"Yes. I promise." He wanted to wrap his arms around her, kiss her, keep her close. But he had never kissed her when he was her brother, and wasn't sure he should start now.

He pulled the flower from his buttonhole and gave it to her. Some of his longing was in his voice. "Good-bye, Eugenie."

"Good-bye."

He could feel her watching him as he walked away.

Too restless to return to the *Jambalaya*, he strode to the end of Decatur Street. He walked on and on, past a closed market square.

Beyond that, there was a public park built around a pretty lake. He sat on a bench and watched a boy feeding bread to some ducks. A little girl was trying to grab the bread, shrilling at him, "Why won't you let me take a turn?"

A placid pair of swans glided over the water. People strolled on the paths, peaceful on this lovely afternoon.

Suddenly there was a loud boom. The ground shook. The swans fluttered. The ducks squawked and flew away.

"What was that?" the children asked each other.

Startled, people looked toward the river. It was several miles away, but the noise had come from that direction.

"Sounded like an explosion," a man said.

Jonathan jumped to his feet, chilled by premonition. He heard the clanging of fire bells. He ran from the park and tried to get his bearings, to find the quickest way through town. The late afternoon sky seemed to darken with his dread.

At last he reached the river road, and saw the *Jambalaya* half a mile or so away, a couple of fire engines on the road near it, the docks swarming with people. Smoke rose from the boat. As Jonathan ran near, he saw a gaping hole in the deck. The wood around it seemed charred. Fire hoses were soaking it with long streams of water. He couldn't tell if it was still burning.

He finally reached the dock, and was caught in the swirl of confusion. He saw Kyle, and shouted at him, "What happened?"

"The tank of acetylene gas—under the stage—it blew up—probably a gas leak—"

"Step aside, please." A fireman moved past Jonathan.

He managed to reach Nettie and Farley. They were standing together, looking at the *Jambalaya* with distraught faces.

"Was anybody on board?" he asked them.

"Just Gus," Nettie answered, and burst into tears.

"Gus? But—where is he?"

Nettie pointed to a tight circle of people. Jonathan saw Velma kneeling beside someone on the ground. He couldn't tell who it was, but realized it must be Gus.

An eternity seemed to pass before a fireman gave

a signal to turn off the hoses. Hyacinth asked, "Is the fire out?"

"Yes," somebody said.

Velma rose and pushed through the crowd. The captain stepped forward and took her arm.

Jonathan could tell by her white face that Gus was dead.

Few of the cabins on the *Jambalaya* had been damaged, but the theater had been largely destroyed. Gus, who had been sitting at the piano right in front of the exploding tank, had lived less than an hour. If he had been somewhere else on board, he might not have been hurt.

Captain Farrell arranged to have him buried in a little cemetery in Petit's Landing. Still stunned by the tragedy, the troupe gathered there for the graveside service. Heartsick, Jonathan thought of Gus's big ambitions, his determined practicing of "Sugartown Stomp." He could almost see him at the piano, the cigar clenched between his teeth. Maybe he had struck a match to light it—

After the service, the troupe dispersed. Many were weeping.

Velma stopped Jonathan, putting something in his hand. "My dear, Gus asked me to give you this."

"What is it?"

"His wallet. It has his train ticket in it, and the money he saved."

Jonathan was bewildered. "I don't understand."

Velma fought for control. "He knew he was dying when—when they carried him off the boat." There was a shadow of that horror in her eyes, but she continued evenly, "He told me he wanted you to have this ticket. And the money. And—the chance to go."

"But—"

"Take it, Jonathan. You can exchange the ticket for another date. Go in a week or two, or whenever you're ready to leave. We'll—" Her voice broke. "We'll all be here for a while."

That afternoon Jonathan hired a buggy and rode to the railway station in Laitue. He hadn't been in this town since he had stepped off the Orphan Train five years ago. He hitched the horse by the station and walked up the street, toward the meetinghouse.

He remembered the rain on that day, and the ragged line of children . . . Binch, Roy, Kyle . . . Marguerite . . . the toddlers . . . the boy who had sat beside him on the train . . . Eugenie, spunky and scared in her wrinkled stockings . . . and himself, the boy he had been.

He felt again the vague, fragile hopes he had clung to then.

He stopped in front of the meetinghouse door, and looked at it for a long, long time.

Then he returned to the railway station. He gave the train ticket to the agent at the window. "I want to turn this in, please."

"Exchange or refund?"

"Refund."

The agent gave him the full price of the ticket. Jonathan put it carefully in Gus's wallet. He got into his hired buggy and rode slowly back to Petit's Landing.

The sun was low in the sky when he reached the town. The damaged showboat bobbed idly at its mooring. Boxes of ruined props and costumes had been unloaded onto the dock. Weary and disheveled, a few members of the troupe stood there sadly, along with scattered groups of townspeople. Nettie held the whimpering Doodah in her arms.

Jonathan was too numb to think, but seeing the beginnings of a crowd, he boarded the showboat. It still smelled of burnt paint and charred wood. From his cabin he got his tin whistle and the lucky derby hat Gus had given him long ago.

He returned to the dock, cocked the hat on his head, and began to play "Marching Through Georgia."

For a minute, no one moved. Then Kyle ran on

board and got his pie plates, clashing them together like cymbals.

Farley Sander was next up the gangplank. Returning with his baton, he twirled it skillfully as he marched in place near Jonathan.

The new comic, who had inherited Charlie Bolind's tuba, appeared with it, and a rousing *oompah-pah* was added to the song. Then there was the boom of a bass drum, and the toot of a trumpet.

More and more townspeople gathered. They pressed nearer, watching and listening.

After several pieces, Jonathan closed the informal concert by saying, "We'll finish with the song Gus Gessel always ended with." He led the players in "Dixie."

When the last note had died away, there was a moment of silence. Then a black man at the edge of the dock called softly, "Pass the hat, Mr. Dale."

Surprised, Jonathan walked over and handed him the derby. The black man put a coin in it, saying, "For the *Jambalaya*." He passed the hat to the man next to him, who also dropped in some change. "For the *Jambalaya*."

Each person in the crowd put money in the hat, repeating the words.

When the derby was returned to Jonathan, it was spilling over with coins. He walked with it to where

Velma stood alone, her back straight, her eyes glittering with tears.

"For you." Jonathan put the derby in her hands. On top of the other money, he placed Gus's bulging wallet. "For the *Jambalaya*."

He knew she and the captain needed it, and someday he would get to New York on his own.

Someday . . .

·{ **About This Book** }·

In the first half of the nineteenth century, tens of thousands of homeless children lived on the streets of New York City. Many had been orphaned by cholera, typhoid, and influenza epidemics that swept the city. Others were victims of the crushing poverty and overcrowdedness of New York slums, abandoned by families who could not take care of them. The young vagrants slept in alleys and doorways, or wherever they could find shelter. Some became newspaper boys or bootblacks, or survived as beggars or pickpockets. Large numbers of them were arrested and confined in adult prisons.

Shocked by the conditions in which these children were struggling to exist, Charles Loring Brace, one of the founders of the Children's Aid Society in New York, devised a "placing-out" system in 1854. His plan was to send homeless children on special trains to rural areas of the country, where their labor was needed on farms and in small businesses.

Local agents were supposed to check the suitability of people applying for a child, but mistakes were made.

Some children were virtually enslaved or abused by the people who took them in. Young runaways drifted from one foster home to another.

But many Orphan Train riders settled in good homes, and became responsible members of their new families and communities. It is a tribute to their strength and spirit that they overcame the hardships of their early lives, and moved on to a better future.

Between 1854 and 1929, more than a hundred thousand children traveled the Orphan Trains. It was the largest mass relocation of children in United States history.

E.S.H.

ELIZABETH STARR HILL says, "My own performing experience gave me a lasting love of the theater and its history. In *Broadway Chances* and *The Street Dancers*, I wrote about Clement Dale and his show business family. Now, in *The Banjo Player*, Clement's grandfather, Jonathan Dale, takes center stage!"

Ms. Hill is the author of many books for young readers, including *Broadway Chances*, an *American Bookseller* "Pick of the Lists"; *The Street Dancers*; *Evan's Corner*, an ALA Notable Book; and *When Christmas Comes* (all Viking and Puffin). Born in the rural South, she now lives in New Jersey.